in search of LOVE

Piyushi Dhir

Love

in search of LOVE

Piyushi Dhir

pblishing.com
write • share • connect • publish

In Search of Love *by* Piyushi Dhir

Published in 2016 by www.pblishing.com

Marketed by

Maple Press Private Limited
Sales Office A 63, Sector 58, Noida 201 301, U.P., India
phone +91 120 455 3581, 455 3583
email info@**maple**press.co.in
website www.**pblishing**.com

ISBN: 978-81-93271-12-4

Cover, Typesetting, and Book Design by **Flying Trees Private Limited**
Printed in India

10 9 8 7 6 5 4 3 2 1

dedicated to

Love

Table of Contents

Prologue

Ayesha is a young travel-writer, who has been stumbling along in her search for love. Nursing a broken heart, she decides to visit her parents in Ahmedabad for a short reprieve. Even as she struggles to resign herself to a marriage 'arranged' by her parents, she runs into their neighbour's attractive son.

Parth is more than happy to spend time in his own company, in the comforts of his 'resort'. His plan to take some time off before he plunges head long into his career lands him in front of a lovely girl. The pain in her eyes belies her warm smile and he finds himself irresistibly drawn to her. Yet he knows that this cannot end well, for any intimacy with her is forbidden.

Fate plays a cruel trick with Ayesha when it ends her search for love in a cul-de-sac, a point of no return. Ayesha is distraught when she realises that the one person she has finally fallen in love with, is not hers to be had.

They part ways with memories that will return to haunt them and questions that will remain unanswered, until another tryst, seven years later on the other side of the world.

chapter

1

Parth was waiting at the Centraal Station to take a train back home, when he was shaken out of his reverie.

The train was moving slowly, coming to a halt at his stop and in one of the compartments that had just gone by, he thought he had seen her. Was he imagining this too? It wouldn't be the first time after all. In the early days of their parting ways, Parth had seen her face in many other faces. With time, that had gradually ceased.

As the train came to a halt, he hopped on through the door closest to him and made his way towards the compartments in the front. Even as he excused himself and walked on inside the train, he wondered if she would even want to see him. She may have moved on. She would be married by now. It had been seven years. In fact, a quick calculation told him that at the age of 32, she could even have children by now. All the same, he could not stop himself.

He walked through three compartments and was moving on to the fourth when he spotted her. She was seated a couple of rows ahead and he could see the reflection of her face in the train windows. He had not been mistaken. He had known this face for six days only, but he could not have forgotten it for the rest of his life. She was immersed in a book.

His heart thudded as he observed her from where he was standing. It took him a couple of minutes to tear his eyes away from the face he had craved to see for so long. There was a man sitting next to her, but he looked Dutch. Could she be married to a local here?

Should he approach her?

Fifteen minutes on, Parth had not made a move. He looked at her longingly, but something made him hold back.

She was leaning her head against the window of the train and a lock of hair fell across her face. Parth imagined himself bending over and gently tucking her hair behind her ear, just as he had done all those years back. Memories flooded back and brought a pained smile to his face.

She put her book into her bag, collected her belongings and moved towards the door. It was now or never. Parth followed her off the train and onto the road. As she set up a brisk pace, Parth found himself trailing, still unsure about what to do. He tried to form some words in his mind, but nothing seemed right.

Suddenly, she whirled around to face him. She must have sensed someone following her. She was about to open her mouth to tell him off, when her jaw dropped. She had recognised him!

He saw a volley of emotions pass through her eyes-surprise, anger, sadness and finally, a resigned look. They stood like that for a few minutes, until Parth closed the distance between them.

"Ayesha..."

She stared back. He thought he saw tears in her eyes, but she blinked them back hastily and looked away.

"Would you like to take a walk with me?"

She was silent for a minute, after which she nodded imperceptibly. He considered taking her hand in his, but decided not to. He started walking in the direction she had taken and she turned around and followed.

After a few moments of silence, Parth turned to look at her as she walked beside him. He was reminded of the strolls they had taken together in the moonlight. She hadn't changed much, but the vivaciousness he had known in her all those years back, seemed to have receded. She seemed sad and he wondered if he had pained her by showing up suddenly.

"So, how have you been?" he asked gently.

"Fine, thanks. How come you're here?" Ayesha found her voice finally.

"I'm working here."

"With the same company you were to join when we'd met last?"

"No, I worked with them for a while. Then switched jobs and moved here a couple of years ago."

They reached a pretty café alongside a canal and Parth suggested they sit there. He wanted to be able to see her face. They took a table for two on the pavement outside the café. The lamp hanging above their table shed a soft glow on her face. Parth watched her profile as she gazed at the lights reflecting in the water of the canal.

He could hardly believe he was here. Just an hour ago, he had been strolling in Vondelpark, thinking about her. He had been in the office all day and had needed to get some fresh air. Leaving his workplace at around 8pm, he had taken the path along a little lake within the park, watching tiny Dutch kids zoom by on roller skates. The light in the sky had not faded. The first time he had landed in Amsterdam, it was a similar time of the year, and he had been quite startled to discover that it did not turn dark before 10pm in the summer months.

Parth had been in no mood to return home. He could foresee a lonely evening on the couch, eating something he would quickly put together. In his 20s, he had been a loner, who was happiest by himself in his own surroundings. Now, as he was approaching the age of 35, he was beginning to crave for companionship. Not so much the noisy camaraderie with his office colleagues when they went out to catch a soccer match together, but more of the quiet, comfortable companionship of a loved one, with whom he could share the little things in life.

That is when he had thought about her.

"So, what is it like, working here?" Ayesha asked.

His thoughts wandered back to earlier in the day. Parth worked for a reputed beverages behemoth and his job was no doubt comfortable and well-paying, but was beginning to get a little monotonous. He had loved his early days of employment in India, when he had worked hands-on in the factory. Never one to shy away from work, Parth had often laboured ceaselessly for more than 24 hours in the plant. The production lines, of course, never stopped, and every moment he spent away from them left him restless.

He had quickly gained the respect of the other workers, even though he was younger than them in age. Parth had in him the right mix of humility and responsibility: humility, which allowed him to learn from the workers who were more experienced than him, and responsibility, which ensured he never shied away from taking tough decisions.

His ability to take ownership, even when things went wrong, earned him his co-workers' admiration soon enough. A couple of new ideas proposed by him had led to some historic achievements on the production lines and he had never looked back after that.

From India, he had moved to Malaysia and then Amsterdam, switching companies and growing fast through the hierarchy. He was in the strategy team and felt empowered knowing that decisions taken by his team impacted the company and its customers across the globe. But this growth had taken him away from what he loved the most- the greasy action-packed factory life. His passion for his job had taken away a lot more from his life, but that was something he preferred not to dwell upon.

"Not so bad. What about you? What is it like for you?"

"Not so bad either," she flashed him a smile.

Their eyes met and for a minute, neither could turn away. Then the moment passed and Ayesha turned to look back at the water.

Just like the old days, they both sat in silence, each contemplating their own thoughts. Ayesha was carried back to that fateful summer seven years ago, which had changed her life in ways she could never have imagined.

chapter

2

"Wednesday is an auspicious day for new beginnings. You must meet him that day."

"Yes, Ma," Ayesha sighed, resigned to her Mother's unrelenting efforts at finding her a suitable husband.

Mrs Savita Khanna beamed in pleasure at what she saw as another step towards the completion of her maternal duties. She had just finished scanning the Matrimonial Section of the Sunday Times, and left a few ads circled to be followed up this week. Anant Puri, a result of last week's matrimonial search, was the boy she wanted Ayesha to meet once she returned to Delhi.

Mrs Khanna had already contacted Anant's parents, and was quite satisfied with the bio-data and pictures she had received. A cardiac surgeon at the esteemed Adonis Hospital in Delhi, Anant was 26 years old, 5'10" in height and from a well-educated family of doctors. Mrs Khanna was quite convinced that she had found a '*heera*', a diamond, for her daughter and would be thanked for it for the rest of her life.

Col. Prakash Khanna sat quietly on the breakfast table, busy with his newspaper, but he hadn't missed a word of the conversation. Very fond of his only daughter, he had often told Ayesha not to feel pressurised into accepting an arranged marriage. He had clarified that they would be very willing to meet and get to know any boy she chose for herself. He glanced at her for a second before returning his eyes to the article on Sachin Tendulkar's long-due 100th century.

Ayesha, done with her breakfast, excused herself and went upstairs to her room, reflecting on the same thing her father had been thinking about, just moments ago. She was unsure about the entire system of an 'arranged marriage'. Yet, she didn't have the courage to search for her own love. She had tried in the last few years and ended up with a broken heart - thrice! That was enough to put her in severe doubt about her ability to judge people correctly.

Nor was she ready to completely hand over the task of searching for her life-partner to her Mother. How could she be sure that the person her Mother selected as the best for her, didn't turn out to be a total psychopath post-marriage? After all, how much do you get to know of a person in a few weeks' acquaintanceship?

Perplexed by these thoughts, she strolled onto the terrace attached to her room. She had only arrived this morning and had come to this new home for the first time. Having recently retired from the Army, Col Prakash Khanna had lately acquired and moved into this duplex in Ahmedabad, as this was his last place of transfer.

Ayesha loved spending time with people, but loved her privacy as much, and was quite pleased to discover that she had the only room upstairs completely to herself. Along with the terrace, the upper floor of the house was her haven.

As she strolled, she peered at the neighbouring house, with its own terrace separated from hers only by a low wall, about two feet in height. Adventurous by nature, she began nursing a plan to jump the wall and explore her neighbour's terrace by night, when everyone would surely be asleep.

From what her Mother had told her, there was only a middle-aged couple in that magnificent house. The Mehta's must be well-off, she mused, judging by the palatial look of their mansion. Due to the limited size of the plot on the side closer to the Khanna's home, the houses had been built with a common wall in between, thus resulting in a shared roof.

Ayesha sighed as she remembered the appointment her Mother had fixed for her next Wednesday. She had a week here in Ahmedabad before she returned to join her office on Monday. Kabir, her boss, had allowed her a week off in lieu of the recent travel-assignment she had taken on. It had been quite hectic and the break was a well-deserved one.

A travel-writer by profession, Ayesha's job was not as glamorous as it sounded to most. Action-packed schedules demanded that she see and review at least three, sometimes four cities, in as many days, which meant she barely had time to sleep or actually enjoy the sights and sounds.

A restless person by nature, Ayesha was not complaining. She knew that she would rather work in a frenzied manner on the move, than be stuck at a permanent desk for fixed hours every day. The very thought of spending 12 hours day after day on one unmoving desk gave her shudders!

~~❖~~

"Yes Kavita, a Doctor at Adonis," averred Ayesha. She was strolling on the terrace in the moonlight, updating her childhood friend about Mother's latest catch in the marriage market. Kavita, an unusually non-rebellious girl for today's age, had unquestioningly submitted to an arranged marriage when told to do so by her parents.

Kavita came from a particular business-class section of Indian society, which was famed for marrying their children off amongst themselves, more with an eye on furthering business interests than on ensuring compatibility. She had grown up knowing this and somehow never thought of questioning it or trying to alter her fate. Fortunately for her, Vikrant, her husband, turned out to be a mature and understanding man who offered her a secure marriage with adequate affection, if not passion.

Kavita, as a result, had no reason to believe that an arranged marriage was less preferable to one that stemmed from love. This was exactly what she was trying to explain to Ayesha. She knew her friend well enough to know that Ayesha was quite likely to do the opposite of what she was told, more for the sake of being independent than because she truly believed her choice was better. For this very reason, she feared that Ayesha would refuse to see Anant, even though by the sound of it, he seemed to be a very eligible young man.

"Ayesha, there's no harm in seeing him. And in any case, I think he is in a very noble profession!" Kavita added as an afterthought, hoping that at least this would turn the die in favour of the new boy.

"Ka!" Ayesha gave in with a giggle. "Okay, a short meeting, but I promise nothing."

"That's all right. We'll take a call after you've seen the guy. For all you know he'll be so handsome, you won't be able to take your hands off him!"

Ayesha laughed in delight at her dear friend's naughty bent of mind, and wondered for the millionth time how such a girl could have so tamely given in to being married off to a boy she had only spoken to for five minutes before the wedding.

As they bid each other sweet dreams (and on Kavita's insistence, 'Anant-dreams'), Ayesha wondered if she was placing too much importance on searching for her own life partner. After all, things had worked out just fine for Kavita, and may even do so for her. She just needed to trust her parents' choice and given the results of her own disastrous choices earlier, it should not be too difficult to do so.

As she reached one edge of the roof and turned around, Ayesha was startled at the sight of a shadow less than a few feet away. On closer observation, she realised there was a young man sitting on the narrow wall between the two adjoining houses. As she resumed her strolling, she realised with a frown that the boy was actually grinning at her. She stubbornly refused to acknowledge the cheeky fellow and stared straight ahead of her as she walked on, but was keenly aware of his eyes following her.

"I think you should meet this fellow. Anant, is it?" the boy addressed her directly.

Chagrined, she whirled around and said with all the sarcasm she could muster, "Thanks a ton for your invaluable advice. I wonder what I would have done without it!"

He laughed warmly and for a second, she softened towards him. She stood with her hands on her hips and stared at him, wondering at his audacity.

"Hi! I'm Parth," he declared as he extended his hand towards her. She hesitated for a moment, but then felt a little foolish about not acknowledging the hand of friendship that remained suspended in the air. She finally closed the gap between them and shook hands with him.

"I'm Ayesha."

"Mm... Ayesha... Nice name."

They stood there for a minute in silence while she

wondered the inevitable question: who was he? Her parents were asleep and she was all alone on the terrace. Should she be worried? But he had a very endearing smile that put her at ease.

"So you've been overhearing my conversation?" she finally broke the silence.

"Mm... Difficult not to. And you can't blame me. I was just sitting on my own terrace innocently."

"Yeah right!" After a pause, "So you live in this house?" she asked, pointing at the Mehta's mansion.

"No, I'm just hopping over all roofs in Ahmedabad today. Want to join me?"

Ayesha laughed out and stood looking at this boy who sounded so flippant and yet, there was something so sincere in his eyes. She continued, "Actually, I've come home for the first time today itself and am not yet familiar with the city, or even the neighbours for that matter!"

"I can see that. I could show you around if you'd like that."

"We'll see about that. As of now, all I know about you is that your name is Parth and you hop around on Ahmedabad's terraces by night."

This time, it was he who laughed out loud. Ayesha liked the way his hair flopped onto his forehead a bit. He was either due for a haircut or liked having his wavy hair fall onto his head. Always having seen crisp crew-cuts in the Army, overgrown hair was something she couldn't help but notice.

"All I know about you is that your name is Ayesha and you're supposed to meet Dr Anant in Delhi next week. That didn't stop me from offering to show you around!"

"So how long have you been in Ahmedabad?" she changed the subject.

"From the time I was born, except for the last five years or so, when I've been out for studies."

"And now?"

"Well, I have landed a decent job. I'm due to join in two months' time, so I'm home till then."

"Nice! So where were you studying?"

"Why does this sound like an interview to me? Marriage interview?" he asked with a wink.

"Why? Are you interested?" she shot back.

"Are you?"

"Do you ever give straight answers?" she asked in mock exasperation.

She looked up at the moon and his eyes followed hers. As they stood in silence, she admired the moon as she had a million times before. She shared a curious companionship with it. A romantic at heart, she had often thought while watching it that her Mr Right, whoever he was and wherever he was, might also be looking at it at the very same time as her.

She looked back at Parth and asked, "Can you see a face in the moon?"

"Can you?"

"Hmm... I often wonder if I'm crazy. Isn't that something we tell children? That you can see a face in the moon...."

"It is said to be a sign of creativity."

She smiled and looked at him. "That's quite reassuring."

"So, are you?"

"Am I what?"

"Are you creative?"

"I don't know. Maybe. I do write poetry."

"On the moon and moonlight?"

"Not yet, but on many other things."

He looked into her eyes thoughtfully. She looked back wondering what he was thinking.

Her eyes riveted to the moon again. As some words began to formulate in her mind, she whispered them into the night:

"Gently pour upon me your love
Pure and white, soft as a dove
Look at the moon as it looks onto me
Though apart, together we be"

She reluctantly drew her eyes away from her muse, but found Parth still lost in the moon and his thoughts. She waited, uncertain whether to break the moment by making some inconsequential remark. He finally looked back at her. Yet, she felt she didn't have him back completely. He seemed to be elsewhere.

"So now I have written a poem on the moon as well," she tentatively tried regaining the comfortable camaraderie they seemed to have developed just moments ago.

"Mm..."

"I seem to have lost you."

He smiled. After a long moment, he asked on a completely different note, "So what do you do? You live in Delhi it seems."

"Yes, I graduated from there and then joined 'Rolling Stones'. It's a travel and tourism company. I work as a travel-writer for them."

"That sounds quite interesting. I don't think I know any other travel-writer. So do you enjoy your work?"

"Oh yes, I am quite a restless person. And with Papa being an Army man, I have grown into the habit of a nomadic life. Now even though I'm settled in one city, my profession allows me to explore and discover new places. Plus, I like writing. But now I feel like I'm the one being interviewed!"

They both laughed at that together. Noting that she had been standing all this while, Parth invited her to perch on the ledge too. She had no reason to refuse, and she couldn't deny to herself that she was enjoying his company. He seemed rather relaxed and made her feel at ease.

She did, however, hope that he would not mistake her easy affability for anything more, for that was a problem she seemed to get caught in a little too often. Ayesha had always been a warm and friendly girl and many boys had incorrectly assumed her to be 'romantically' interested in them, if she displayed the slightest sign of friendliness.

With the recent disasters in her personal life, the last thing she wanted right now was any kind of romantic involvement. In fact, she had vowed to stay away from the entire male species and just focus on her work. Yet she wasn't sure how true she would be able to stay to her self-made promise, for even though Ayesha wasn't searching for love at the moment, she couldn't stop herself from making friends.

That was probably what had drawn her to Parth too, and allowed her to sit and converse with a complete stranger. Thinking of how easily they had fallen into a light banter, she suddenly remembered that it had all begun with Parth overhearing her conversation with Kavita. So he probably did think that she was 'looking-out'! This thought made her a little uncomfortable.

To add to her discomfiture, she wondered what her Mother would have to say about her sitting on the rooftop past midnight with a guy she had met for the first time less than half an hour ago and of whom she knew little more than his name.

Sensing her thoughts, Parth gently enquired, "Would you like to return indoors now? It's quite late."

Though Ayesha was enjoying their companionship, she felt it would be wise to not stretch this adventure too long, lest her parents come up on the roof accidentally and misunderstand what they see.

"I guess I should turn in now."

Parth nodded, simultaneously swinging his legs onto her side of the terrace. Startled, she looked at him, wondering what he had understood!

Had she, by any chance, indicated that "they" should turn in together now?!

"So Miss Ayesha, may I drop you off to your door?"

Relieved and flattered at the same moment, Ayesha allowed herself a broad grin and replied, "Off course, Mr Parth. It would be a pleasure."

As they walked towards her door, she enquired, "So is this chivalry?"

"Mm... There are a lot of ghosts and demons around at this time. It's not safe for a pretty, young girl to be walking around unescorted."

She blushed at the concealed compliment and looked down shyly.

In a minute, they reached the doorstep of her room. Unwilling to let him go, but unsure of his intentions, she stepped in. “Goodnight Parth.”

He looked into her eyes and she could have sworn for a minute that he could read her thoughts. Then, with a quick wave, he turned around and headed back.

chapter 3

Early next morning the Khanna's drove towards the famous Akshardham temple on the outskirts of the city. Since Ayesha was visiting Ahmedabad for the first time, her parents had decided to show her around. With her unending interest in discovering new cities, Ayesha was happy to be out and about. She speculated on what Kabir would have to say to her doing an article on Ahmedabad, combined with Gandhinagar and a place or two around. She could probably use it as an excuse to come home the next time.

On the long drive out of the city, Ayesha found her thoughts wandering back to the previous night's rendezvous on her terrace. She half-wondered how much of it had been real, and whether she had dreamt up some of it. She was mildly surprised to note that her thoughts had automatically brought a smile to her face. There was something about this boy- she marveled at the way she had felt so warm and comfortable in his presence.

The mention of Parth by her mother in the front of the car brought her zipping back to reality.

"... with the name of Arjuna or Partha or something like that; some Mahabharata-inspired name. She had said that he was to arrive yesterday. We should probably drop in and say a hello. I did try to enquire whether they were looking for a match for him. He is very suitable for our Ayesha. At 27, he is just the right age, being 3 years older than her; foreign-returned and well-placed in a job; and of course, the family is very nice and well-off too. Imagine, Ayesha married off in the house right next-door, won't that be nice?"

Ayesha didn't think so, but refrained from expressing her thoughts aloud. She imagined a situation like that would leave her quite sandwiched between two sets of parents.

"But Mrs Mehta was elusive about her plans for his marriage. Either he is already committed elsewhere or they aren't planning his marriage anytime soon," Mrs Khanna continued.

Ayesha didn't know whether to feel relieved or disappointed. She was relieved that there would be no immediate pressure to meet him, decide and give an answer. But she was also disappointed because...

Actually, she didn't know why she should feel disappointed! Yes, he was good looking, had a very endearing smile, and a flop of unruly hair that she liked. She felt at ease with him, but it wasn't like she had been thinking beyond that.

Or had she?

Though it was a weekday, there was a reasonably long line outside the temple. Ayesha noticed that not all of the people in the queue looked like tourists. In fact the majority of the visitors seemed to be from surrounding villages and towns. For many of them, this was probably a notable event, for they were decked up in finery. The women wore their better looking *sarees*, girls sported imitation jewelry and the little ones were fit into frothy frocks and fancy jeans.

By the time they got past the stringent security check, the sun was well up in the sky. Ayesha took her *dupatta* over her head to save her face from the stark sun. She was dressed in a white *kurti* and white *churidar*, with a multi-coloured bright dupatta and a range of coloured glass bangles.

They deposited their footwear at the assigned counter and headed for the temple stairs. Ayesha strained to walk on the hot stone while peeping out of her dupatta so as not to ram into someone, and suddenly stopped! She was probably seeing a mirage in the heat. Or was that really Parth?!

Her mother had seen Mrs Mehta too by then and was walking straight towards her. Ayesha followed slowly, wondering at the astonishing co-incidence. The two ladies hugged and exclaimed, while the men-folk serenely exchanged pleasantries. Ayesha looked up curiously at Parth and found him smiling at her just as if they were all alone on the terrace again. She instantly lowered her eyes and stood close to her mother, who began making the introductions.

When Parth and Ayesha were presented to each other, they just nodded like strangers. Greatly relieved that he had not shown any visible sign of recognition, Ayesha conceded him a quick glance and found him looking straight into her eyes. In that moment, it was like they had just created and shared their own little secret world that only the two of them inhabited.

The two families entered the famous temple together. As the two ladies got engrossed in completing the rituals and the men discussed the upcoming elections, Ayesha found herself walking along side Parth.

"So, slept well?" he asked her.

"Ohh yes! Thanks! It feels nice not to have to wake up to an alarm. What about you?"

"I'm a creature of the night. I sleep in the morning."

"What time?"

"Mm... around 7 A.M."

"7 A.M.?!" Ayesha was startled. "But that's completely topsy-turvy! And what time do you typically wake up?"

Parth laughed. "Well, that completely depends on whether

I have some work during the day or if my parents have any plans for me. Though if there's nothing in particular, I would wake up for lunch around 2 PM or 3 PM."

"Gosh! That's crazy! And your Mother tolerates that? Mine would throw me out if I tried something like that... Moreover," she added as an afterthought, "I'm barely able to keep my eyes open beyond 10 or 11 in the night."

"Oh, but then when are we going to hop across the terraces of Ahmedabad?"

They both laughed at that. Somehow, under the broad sunlight, the thought now seemed even more absurd than it had the previous night.

"So what do you do all night?" Ayesha was curious.

"I'll show you. Meet me at the same place tonight?"

Ayesha didn't get a chance to answer as the two ladies returned just then. The families stepped out and after bidding each other goodbye, went their own ways. Ayesha regretted not having been able to answer Parth, but wondered at the same time whether she would after all meet him that night.

chapter

4

Sitting in her room late that night, Ayesha cried.

For some inexplicable reason, she was suddenly reminded of Tushar and had been unable to sleep. It had been nine months since they had parted ways, but she still shed tears every time she thought of him. Tears, mixed with anger.

He had made her very happy. Just when she had been trying to cope with the end of her previous relationship, Tushar had walked into her life and taken her in his arms. He had loved her so much. Yet, after the first few months, he had turned cool and then cold, almost as rapidly as they had fallen in love.

She had desperately tried to hold onto him as he moved further and further away from her. She had asked him many times what it was that was changing between them. He had not been able to give her an answer. She finally forced herself to realise that it was over. All she was managing to hold on to was the ghost of a person who no longer existed.

She had been angry- at how easy it was for him to walk away, while life seemed to come crumbling down around her.

She had despaired- at the thought that something was wrong with herself, for her relationships did not last.

She had been desperate- calling him frantically and reminding him of all the happy times they had had together, until he stopped taking her calls.

Now all she had was happy memories, scarred by a miserable end and occasional bursts of poetry through which she tried to vent out her agony.

Hand in hand we walked along
Our love, our bond... it was so strong

IN SEARCH OF LOVE

Heaven, for me, you brought down on this earth
Our union was, for me, a new birth.
Pain, sorrow, hurt... no more.
A flood of love came knocking at my door.

Drowning in troubles, sinking down
You pulled me out, you wiped my frown.
So much love you began to give
I discovered in you, a reason to live.
Fulfilled, satisfied, cheerful and gay
I was, until... you walked away.

Shocked and shattered, I could only weep.
Day after day, I cried myself to sleep.
Why did you go? Why did you leave?
Why did you love me if you had to cleave?

My faith, my trust... broken once again
A burst of love and back to my old pain.
Bewildered and hurt, to think I pause
But try as I might, I find no cause.

Why rescue me, then leave me ashore?
Be there for me and suddenly no more?
Why wipe my tears? Why touch me to the core?
If you had to leave me in pain once more?
Why love me so much? Why make me care?
If you had to walk away leaving me threadbare?
Why? O why? My heart still cries...
No matter how much reason tries...

Each moment of wait proved futile,
New hopes are born... crushed after a while.
You're not coming back... I know. I do.
But my silly heart... it's waiting for you...

Tears poured onto the diary in which she wrote. She shut it and sat up, furious at herself for making such a mess of her life. He didn't deserve her tears. No one did. She brushed away the wetness on her cheeks and promised herself that a good man awaited her somewhere.

In the very same minute, she felt disgusted that she should be consoling herself over one man with the thought of another. Why think of men at all? The previous ones hadn't been any better. They were all like this- you just couldn't trust them. Moody, unreliable cheats!

She washed her face and strolled out to the terrace to get some fresh air. In the warring mood that she was, she hoped Parth wouldn't run into her today, lest he come at the receiving end of her annoyance against the entire male species.

He wasn't there.

She found herself feeling disappointed. Then her anger turned to herself, for sparing even an iota of thought on another man.

She sighed and settled down on the ledge where they had sat the previous night. Absorbed with the moon once again, she pondered about the men in her life. From as far back as she could remember, she had always had friends among boys only. A tomboy back in her childhood, she had never been able to identify much with delicate girls and their doll-like interests.

While other girls of her grade would sit in the shade and gossip amongst themselves during any free period in school, Ayesha would always be found on the basketball court or football ground roughing it out with the boys.

Even now if she thought back, her thickest buddies had all been from the opposite gender. Many of them had fallen for her too, no doubt. And thereafter, the happy stories spiraled downwards. She felt bereft and wondered for the nth time whether there was something wrong with her and the way she dealt with her relationships.

"Lost in Anant's thoughts?" Parth's voice reached her ears like music. He settled down on the ledge too, leaving enough distance between them not to cause her any discomfort. Ayesha was surprised at how glad she was to see him.

"Parth..."

"Mm...?"

"I'm glad you're here. I was feeling lonely."

"You look a little low today. How can we cheer you up? Let's go for a drive."

"A drive? At this time?! Its past 1am!!"

"Perfect! That's exactly why. We can't quite go out for a drive in the middle of daylight, right? Just you and me... I wonder what your mother would have to say to that."

Ayesha burst out laughing at the thought.

"She would start planning our marriage."

"She's obviously in a hurry to get rid of you. Do you trouble her a lot?" he teased.

"No, it's just that she wants to see me happily settled. By the way, she was contemplating you as a potential son-in-law this morning itself. And after seeing you escorting your Mum to the temple like such a good boy, I'm sure it won't be long before she puts up the proposal to your mother."

Parth smiled.

After a few minutes silence, Ayesha finally asked out of curiosity, "Are you seeing someone Parth?"

"Mm... I am."

"Since when?"

"Been about 5 years."

"Wow! That's a long time."

Ayesha took a few moments to let the information sink in and to analyse her feelings. Curiously, she felt no jealousy; only an increased sense of comfort with him. She had had too much emotional upheaval lately to risk another one so soon. Knowing that Parth was committed elsewhere reduced her worries about what his real intentions were as he spent time with her.

"I take it," Parth commented, "that you are not committed."

"You're right."

"Mm... ok."

Ayesha looked back at the Moon and remembered the way Parth had seemed so thoughtful after the few lines she had recited.

"Is it a long-distance relationship?"

"Yup, always been. Started out soon after school, here in Ahmedabad. Then I left for UK. I return after 5 years and now she's working elsewhere."

She nodded.

"So?" Parth asked suddenly.

"So what?"

"So, drive?"

"You're serious about it?"

"Yes, why not?, "Parth asked. "I have promised to show you around, haven't I?"

"And how do you propose we go out for a drive?"

Parth paused while he worked out the plan in his mind, and then asked her, "Can you step out of the house and meet me where this road ends? It's just ten steps from your gate. I'll get the car till then and see you there."

Ayesha wondered if they were seriously discussing a plan as crazy as that. It was close to 2am in the morning. If her parents were to discover that she was missing from the house at any point of time, there was absolutely no plausible excuse she could give. What would she say, "Uhh... I just went out for a drive with the boy next-door at 2 in the morning?!!"

At the same time she found herself quickly taking stock of all the exits of the house. There was one just under the staircase. This door led out into the garage and no one ever used it. Even if her parents did wake up, presuming that they would never come upstairs to check on her, they would not be likely to saunter towards that door hidden away behind brooms and dusters.

"Ok, I'll see you there."

Even as Ayesha speculated whether she had lost her mind, she noticed that Parth too, looked surprised that she had agreed. They looked at each other's expression and started laughing.

"Let's do it!," Parth said.

"Let's do it!," Ayesha agreed.

chapter

5

Ayesha daintily tip-toed down the stairs, holding her slippers in her hands. Once on the ground-floor, she walked around assessing the situation. The door to her parents' room was shut and they seemed fast asleep.

She made her way to the targeted door and found a whole lot of riff-raff piled against it. Piece by piece she moved the brooms, used tube-lights and dusters away from the door, but not so far that it would attract attention. She gently eased the latch open next and prayed the door won't creak. Luck was on her side for the door opened rather smoothly.

Just as she stealthily made her way towards the gate almost ready to sing with joy, she stopped dead in her tracks. There was a huge chain and lock around the gate. She hadn't known that her father locked up the gate every night!

She contemplated jumping over the gate but gave up this option after a minor scrutiny told her she won't manage it too easily. Moreover, if anyone were to see her jumping her own gate at this hour of the night, there was no way the story won't reach her parents the very next morning!

Ayesha realised in despair that she didn't even have Parth's phone number. He would reach the end of the road and wait for her alone there, until he figured that she wasn't coming. As Ayesha started heading back, she had a brainwave. Didn't Papa hang all keys together just inside the entrance of the house?

She tip-toed back into the house and across to the entrance, where she found some seven different keys. With the entire ammunition in her hands and a prayer on her lips, Ayesha went back to the gate. The second key opened the big lock. She could have jumped with joy!

She didn't even bother going back indoors to put the other keys in place. Nor did she spare a thought on what her father would think if he found the gate unlocked. She just fled towards the pre-determined spot.

Her heart still beating at double its usual pace, Ayesha reached the end of the road and found a royal black Mercedes waiting for her. She drew her breath in. She had never sat in anything bigger than her father's Alto! She circled the beauty slowly, admiring it. A tad intimidated, Ayesha opened the door to the passenger seat and got in, afraid that she may commit some sacrilege in this revered object!

The car zoomed off.

Once Parth was sure they were safe and no alarm had been raised yet, he noticed that Ayesha was unusually quiet.

"Is everything all right?"

"Everything, except that I'm terribly nervous right now Parth," she narrated her adventures after they had parted ways on the terrace.

"One brave girl you are. You know, I hadn't actually thought you would do something like this."

"Neither had I!" Ayesha exclaimed.

They both laughed at their madness together.

Slowly Ayesha sat back and relaxed. She had always loved long leisurely drives. She began observing all the endless knobs and screens inside the car.

"Meet Midnight," Parth said to her.

"Ahh! Is that what you call your car?"

"Mm..."

As her eyes roved around, they settled on the sight of the Moon that she could see through Midnight's sunroof. Parth turned to look at her, saw a child-like contentment on her face and smiled to himself.

Just for this, the risk had been worth it.

"By the way Parth, when I was stuck there at the gate and thought I wasn't going to be able to make it today, I realised I don't have your number."

She noted down his number while he recited it and then gave him a call. Since he was driving, she saved her number on his phone too.

"So where are you taking me?"

They had just hit the highway and were heading nowhere in particular.

"Mm... How much time do you have?"

Ayesha glanced at the watch on Midnight's dashboard. 2:17am. "Well, I don't know. The longer I'm out, the more risk I run of being caught. But now that we have made it till here, I don't really feel like getting back."

She sunk back on her seat and Parth drove on. For some time they just shared silence, watching the trees and lamp-posts pass by. After a while Parth glanced at her again.

"Is our adventurous lady asleep?"

"No Parth, this is lovely! I love long drives, you know. Thank you so much!"

"You don't have to thank me. It's totally my pleasure to be driving a pretty lady around in the middle of the night."

"You flatter me too much."

"I'm just saying the truth."

She smiled and they returned to their own respective thoughts. As Ayesha saw them leave behind trees, stones and everything that came on the way, she thought of how she had been crying just a few hours back, and realised that she really needed to let go.

This road was like her life and Tushar had just been a co-passenger for a while. Before she met him, she had been driving along sadly, trying to recover from the previous relationship, where she had found out after a year that the boy she loved had been cheating on her all along.

Tushar had accompanied her for a while on the journey, helping her get over her hurt and bewilderment. She couldn't deny that while he had been with her, she had been very happy. Maybe that had been his purpose in her life. Maybe he was meant to come in for a while, give her support and happiness and then move on. Now she had to accept that and let go.

Parth turned the car around at the next break in the divider. 2:44 a.m. They had been driving for around 30 minutes and it would take them as much time to get back.

Her thoughts wandered back to Tushar. He had left and she was wandering along by herself once again. For some time God had probably sent Parth to accompany her, as he was doing just now. She looked at him and felt glad he was with her. His being in a committed relationship made her feel much at ease, and she looked forward to having a nice friend in him.

Parth turned his head and looked straight into her eyes. They smiled at each other.

"Parth...?"

"Mm...," he said as his eyes reverted to the road once again.

"What is the name of your girl?"

"Naina"

"So how did you meet her, if I may ask?"

"Don't be so formal. Of course you can ask. As I said, I knew her from school. We studied in the same school right from the beginning. I don't even remember when I fell in love. Maybe in Class 7, maybe 5, maybe even earlier. But we started going around only after school got over. Just before I was to leave for the UK."

"Wow! That's an incredible story. You've loved her since you were a kid?! And there's never been anyone else in your life?"

"Nope, never."

"Wooow! I've never heard anything like that!"

Just then Parth turned the car onto the last stretch of road leading back home. He turned the corner and stopped a little distance away from their houses.

"I don't feel like going back...," Ayesha sighed.

Parth reached out and took Ayesha's hand in his. They sat in silence in the quiet calmness of the night.

"So do I see you at the terrace after this?"

"No, Parth. I think I'll sleep now. I have to go out with my parents tomorrow and it's already close to 3:30. I'll probably be half-asleep all day tomorrow and my parents are going to wonder what's wrong with me!"

"Message me once you're back in your room safely," he said.

"I'll do that." Reluctantly, she withdrew her hand from his and opened the door.

As he drove past and she walked the last stretch by herself, her heartbeat shot up in nervousness at the prospect of being found out by her parents while re-entering the house.

She found herself messaging Parth: “I’m super-scared!”

In less than a minute, he replied, “You’ll be just fine. I’m taking care of you.”

She smiled and made her way back home. After locking the gate and hanging the keys back in place uneventfully, she got back upstairs and breathed a sigh of relief. Ayesha had thoroughly enjoyed her midnight adventure, but could still feel the butterflies in her stomach.

She messaged him, “Back in my room, safe and sound. Goodnight Parth.”

By the time she brushed her teeth, washed her face and got into bed, there was a reply from him.

“Goodnight Ayesha.”

When she slept off, a smile was still lingering on her face.

chapter 6

"Ashu," her Mother was nudging her awake. Ayesha barely managed to peek through her eyes and acknowledge her Mother's presence.

"Ashu, you've over-slept. Papa and I are ready. Get ready quickly. What happened? Your alarm didn't ring?"

Oh crap! She had totally forgotten to set the alarm. She jumped out of bed and whizzed around until she was ready 30 minutes later. They left for Old Ahmedabad which was a very crowded area, but nevertheless had some good shops for Gujarati print suits and *lehangas.*

The rest of the morning was spent with the women elatedly bargaining and shopping all over the market, while Col Khanna escorted them around. Once they had stuffed the car with a fair number of shopping bags, they went to Gokula for lunch.

Gokula was known for its extensive spread of unlimited Gujarati food and was popular among the locals and tourists alike. Ayesha loved the sweetened food and the way Gujaratis ate sweets in the middle of their meal! To a rebel like her, who also had a sweet-tooth, it was fascinating to break the otherwise rigid rule of keeping dessert right for the end.

They got back home in time for her to squeeze in an afternoon siesta, which lasted much longer than the afternoon, given her exhaustion from the previous night. She literally dragged herself out of bed at six in the evening and wondered if the rest of her days in Ahmedabad were going to be similarly spent.

~~❖~~

"It's just not fair, Parth! You have the entire day to catch up on sleep! In my part of the world, people wake up early in the morning and expect me to do the same."

They had just been discussing Parth's unusual sleep patterns. He was explaining that his biological clock was still set to UK timings. She however, was complaining that she had to simultaneously inhabit 'his world' during the night and then wake up according to the usual hours in 'her world'.

"...which effectively means I'm trying to straddle two different worlds at the same time!"

"No one's forcing you to."

Ayesha slumped in defeat at this. She couldn't deny that. If she was sitting with Parth on the roof at half past two in the morning, it was purely because she wanted to. No one was compelling her.

"All right, you win!" she conceded.

Parth smiled indulgently. He saw a child in her at times who he was beginning to enjoy pampering. On the other hand, Ayesha could also sound exceedingly mature at times.

They had been sitting on the ledge adjoining the two houses for almost two hours now. He had told her more about Naina and his college life. He had mentioned his sister, Piya, and talked about their relationship. He missed his kid sister. Even after returning to India, they hadn't got much time together as she was studying in Nainital. She was almost ten years younger to Parth.

For someone who was not very voluble, especially about his personal life, he was surprised at the way he was able to open up with Ayesha.

He had just been telling her of how he liked keeping

his room dimly lit, when she had suddenly launched into a spontaneously composed poem on him,

In a solitary planet, all on his own
Dark and dim, prefers to be alone...

Yet there's a girl, whose company he doesn't mind
With her he is all chivalrous and kind

For someone who is usually so quiet
With her he is talkative all right...

"You're quite good at this," he complimented.

"Thank you, thank you! You seem to inspire me to poetry," she returned.

"I've been telling you so much about me. I'll lose all my mysterious charm if I tell you everything. Now you should tell me something about yourself."

"Oh, I'm actually quite happy to be listening to you," she clarified. "You know, it's quite rare for me to be a listener. I'm usually blamed for verbal diarrhea!"

He laughed, and then added, "It's quite rare for me to be the one talking. I'm usually blamed for not having more than monosyllables to add to a conversation."

They were both struck by the incredible rapidity with which they had fallen into such a comfortable friendship with each other.

Parth, who usually took his time choosing friends, was surprised how much at ease he felt talking to Ayesha. Ayesha, who was usually quick to make acquaintances, still marveled at the way, when she was with Parth, she felt like she'd known him forever.

"Won't you tell me anything about your past?" Parth enquired. "I'm sure you haven't lacked admirers."

"You're right, Parth. I definitely have a longer list than you do, but nothing as romantic. I've had a painful past and not one I would like to recollect."

"I definitely don't want you to talk about it then. I like the Ayesha who is so cheerful and adventurous. Up for another adventure tonight?"

With a broad grin on her face, Ayesha asked, "What do you have in mind tonight? Another drive with Midnight?"

"I like the way you've taken to calling him Midnight as well. We could do the drive, but frankly Ayesha, there is a lot of risk involved. I don't want to get you into any kind of trouble."

"Yes, that's true..."

Though it was an appealing option to go for a drive again as she had totally loved it the previous night, Ayesha realised that Parth was being sensible.

"We could try something safer tonight though," Parth ventured.

"Like what?"

"Would you like to drop in and see my dimly-lit room?"

Ayesha looked at him, carefully searching for any questionable motives in his eyes, but realising it was a completely innocent invitation, she relented. He helped her over the ledge and escorted her across his terrace.

"This is a safer option?" Ayesha teased. "What if your parents chance upon us?"

Parth smiled.

Before they took the stairs to his room, she went to the end of the terrace and looked over. There was a large beautiful garden below on what was the front side of his house. There were colourful flowers along the wall and pretty lamp posts that lit up the garden. A thin path wove through the perfectly maintained level grass. From above, the garden looked serene and attractive.

She could sense Parth standing right behind her, looking on to the sight below.

"I call this my resort," he said.

They stood for a while together, admiring this oasis in the middle of an otherwise dull neighbourhood. Just as she was about to turn around, she saw a fleet of cars standing to one side of the garden. Midnight was one among many other luxury cars.

As Parth's social status began sinking in, Ayesha felt curiously distanced from him. She had much preferred the Parth who sat with her on the ledge in his black *pyjamas* and who seemed to be just like her in every respect.

They moved towards the stairs and descended straight into his room. It was, as he had promised, dimly lit by two lamps on either side of his bed. What struck her more, however, was that the room was very simply furnished. Apart from the single bed, there was a table with his laptop, a simple couch and a rack that stored some of his books.

After the lavish spread she had seen below, she felt completely at ease inside this room. Just above his bed, there was a large framed picture of Parth as a kid, laughing playfully in his mother's lap with her arms wrapped around him. One couldn't miss the love between them and it brought a smile to Ayesha's face.

She made herself comfortable on the couch, as she felt it would not be appropriate to sit on the bed. Parth, meanwhile, went to the large window near his bed and looked out at 'his resort'. He seemed quite contented and at peace.

As he stood there in his loose black track pants and a black t-shirt, she marveled at the contradiction of Parth's existence. Being with him right now in this simple, relaxing room, it was difficult to imagine that this boy and this room belonged to the same regal mansion she had just seen from above.

Parth, looking into the distance, was thinking of something else. With the large gap between him and his sister, he had mostly been by himself as a child. He had learnt to keep himself occupied and didn't mind his own companionship.

Even with Naina, he had never spent much time physically together as they had almost always been miles apart, after their relationship had started. Nevertheless, in the last few days, he had grown very used to Ayesha's presence. In fact, when he was not with her, his mind was distracted by thoughts of what she would be doing at that time.

She had unexpectedly entered his life like a breath of fresh air and brightened his 'dim' nights. For someone who had never minded being alone, Parth could feel an impending sense of loneliness descend upon him as he realised that in a few more days Ayesha would be gone. He would be back to his usual nights in 'his resort', but this time, he knew he would definitely feel lonely.

Parth turned to look at this girl whose friendship had suddenly become so dear to him. He found Ayesha curled on his couch, fast asleep. Guilt-ridden by the thought that he was keeping her up long after her usual bed-time, Parth sat on his haunches beside the couch and tried to wake her up.

When calling out her name didn't do much good, he gently held her hand which was tucked close to her face. She shifted a bit, making herself more comfortable and continued to slumber on.

Parth was perplexed. He hadn't ever faced a situation like this!

He tucked a strand of her hair behind her ear and now that he could see her face more clearly, pressed her fingers between his and called out her name again.

"Ayesha, wake up baby. Let's go home. Wake up, c'mon."

She opened her eyes sleepily and attempted to sit up. Parth helped her up, but noticed that she was quite groggy and unsteady.

On an impulse, he picked her up in his arms and started walking up the stairs. She half-protested that she could walk up on her own, but then put her head on his shoulder and settled in. He smiled and carried her over the ledge.

Once they reached her door, he opened it, led her to her bed and tucked her in. She dozed off within seconds, and as her grip loosened around his fingers, he whispered, "Goodnight Ayesha..."

chapter

7

From somewhere deep in her sleep, Ayesha could faintly hear a bell ringing incessantly. Coming closer to reality, she realised it was her phone.

She groped around, still drowsy, until her hands alighted on the handset. Peeking through the smallest possible slit in her eyes, she saw the mobile screen lit up with two words,

Parth calling

"Hlo," she mumbled.

"Ayesha..."

"Hmm...?"

"Girl, its 7 in the morning. You had told me last night that you had an appointment with some doctor at 8. Your parents will be expecting you. I just remembered that you must not have set your alarm last night."

Ayesha sat up groggily trying to make sense of the words she was hearing. As her brain opened its shutters and his words began to sink in, she forced herself awake. Of course, she had an appointment with the dentist and Papa would be expecting her at the breakfast table in half an hour!

"Thank you so much Parth. That was very thoughtful of you. I would have gotten into trouble again. But how come you're up so early?"

"I'm going to sleep now."

"Wow! Crazy you are. Anyway, goodnight then. I'll catch you later. Sleep well!"

"Goodnight Ayesha."

In the shower, once the water began pouring onto her face, her thoughts started clearing and Ayesha recollected the events from the previous night. The 'resort' and the line-up of sedans seemed like a dream now. Parth's comforting room, however, was very much real. She smiled as she remembered how he had carried the sleepy girl back to her room and tucked her into bed.

She marveled at how much she had come to trust him! He was no doubt, very caring and sweet.

Naina was a lucky girl indeed.

~~❖~~

"Are you sure he's completely committed to his girl?" Kavita asked.

Ayesha was out for an evening walk and had just been telling her old friend about her new one.

"Yes, Ka! He looks totally in love when he talks about her. And he's never thought about another girl since he was a kid. Can you believe that?"

"No."

"Uff! You always have to disagree. Believe me. And anyway, I wouldn't spend so much time with him and fall asleep in his room if I had the slightest doubt about his integrity. I totally trust him."

"Good for you. So what does he look like," Kavita asked in her characteristic inquisitive manner.

"He's quite cute actually. Dresses quite simply given that he's so well-off in reality. In fact, that's what I love about him. Being with him, it's so easy to forget that he's actually the owner of a fleet of Mercs and a palatial house. Very down-to-earth and very, very chivalrous."

"You're sure you're not falling for him, right?"

"I am growing very fond of him Ka, but don't worry,

I won't ever steal another girl's man. I only think of him as a very good friend and companion."

"Does she know about you?"

"I don't know, but you definitely sound like one very suspicious woman! Are you as possessive about Vikrant?"

They laughed together and Kavita allowed the conversation to move on. Before hanging up, she asked Ayesha to visit her in Chandigarh, and Ayesha promised she would try.

~~❖~~

Ayesha sat dwindling her pen above a blank page in her diary.

"Yesterday it was Anant. Now today Ma told me to also meet a boy called Saurabh. This guy is an IIT-IIM super-genius combination, currently working with American Express. It sounds so easy to say that I should meet this one and that one. But how do I explain to her that I'm really scared.

I knew Shiven for more than a year and believed in him, until I discovered that he had been cheating on me all along. After that, it was Tushar. How can I meet Anant or Saurabh or anyone else for an hour, maybe two hours, and decide if the boy is apt to be my partner for life?"

She sighed. Then looked out of her window.

Her thoughts moved on to Parth.

How was it that with Parth, she had experienced trust so soon? It was just an instinct, but with him she felt safe. She felt that no matter what, he would never harm her. So was it possible to judge someone correctly in such a short span of time? Or was it that it was easier to have faith when the stakes were not high.

With Parth, after all, there was not much to lose, just the friendship of a few days. With Anant or Saurabh or whoever the guy was going to be, she couldn't afford to trust so easily and then discover she had been wrong. They might be married by the time she realised the truth!

Ayesha forced herself to think of something different. She was tired of worrying about her search for love. She was a strong believer of destiny. Whatever she was destined for would happen to her at any rate, and no amount of worrying was going to change that. Comforted by the thought, she reached out for her phone and messaged,

"Parth......"

"Mm....," he replied.

"Do I see you tonight...?"

"Do you want to see me...?"

He still needed to ask! But then Parth hardly ever gave straight answers.

"Depends on whether you have a nice adventure planned for me tonight," was her SMS back to him.

"Mm... That's a challenge. Let's see. May I pick you up now?"

"I would love that."

Within minutes, there was a soft knock at the door of her room that led out onto the terrace. She slipped out and joined him in the moonlight.

They sat on the ledge together trying to identify constellations. Ayesha always found it easiest to spot the Orion. After she had pointed out its features to Parth, he helped her identify the Big Bear, shaped like a big spoon. They sat like two children, swinging their legs and counting stars.

After a while, Parth took out a chocolate from his pocket and offered it to Ayesha. She was quite delighted and confessed she had a weakness for chocolates.

"So what else do you like?" he asked.

She pondered the question for a while. Then suddenly got up and ran inside to her room.

He was still wondering what he had said that had offended her when she returned with a diary in her hand. She perched back on the ledge, flipped some pages, found what she wanted and read out to him,

Honey and water
A lemon tree
Small little things
That fill me with glee

A fluttering butterfly
Petals of a flower
Drops of dew
A sudden rain-shower

Little boys in shorts
A sleepy puppy
The breeze on my face
A wide vast sea

Floating clouds
Stars in the sky
The droning of a bee
And birds that fly

A stranger's smile
Girls feeling shy
Blushing cheeks
An infant's cry

But most of all
What is beautiful
What warms the heart
And stirs the soul

Is the feeling of love
The sharing of lives
Of pain and joy
Of sorrows and smiles

Parth looked at her wordlessly, marveling at the way she could express herself so well in rhyme. Suddenly self-conscious, she shut the diary and put it aside.

"How many more such poems are hidden away in that diary?, he asked.

"A couple of more."

"Do I get to see them?"

"Maybe... With time... Do you also write?"

"No, but I sketch."

"You do?! You never told me before."

"You never asked."

"Oh Parth! May I see some of them please?"

"Uh huh, come on," he jumped onto his side of the roof and held out a hand to help her over. They made their way down to his room, which was once again dimly-lit. Soft music played on the laptop. She went and sat on his table this time, in the hope that she won't as easily doze off against the hard wood!

Parth went to his cupboard and fetched some large rolled up sheets. He spread them open on the bed and held down the corners with his hands. She slowly stood up from the chair and moved closer to the drawing she saw right at the top.

It was a huge pencil-sketch of a girl staring into the distance. The setting seemed to be rural and the girl was wrapped in a *saree*. Though simple, there was something sensual about the girl; maybe it was the way she had draped the *saree* with a generous glimpse of her shapely curves. She seemed lost in the world of her thoughts.

The next was a sketch of what definitely looked like Midnight. The lines were sharp and it seemed like Midnight was zooming right past you. There were a few more images of cars. It was quite obvious Parth had a fixation for cars and girls, as the next image was again of a girl.

Only this time, the girl looked astonishingly like Ayesha!

The young woman in the image sat staring up at the moon, enraptured by its aura. She was seated on the ground, with her arms wrapped around her legs and her chin on her knees. What she loved most about it was the expression on the girl's face- it was one mixed with wonder, affection and joy, probably the very blend of emotions she herself experienced looking at the moon.

She raised her head and looked at him, but found his eyes on the picture.

Parth rolled up the sheets and carried them back to his cupboard and Ayesha decided to let the moment pass. She began strolling around the room observing this refuge that

Parth retired to every night. The songs playing on his laptop changed to one of her favourites, "*Tum ho toh...*"

She started moving to the beats of the soft, slow song. In a minute, Ayesha was swirling and twirling around the room, uninhibited and just enjoying the rhythm of the song.

Parth, standing to one side, had been watching her with a smile on his face. He took a step ahead and extended his hand in invitation. Ayesha put her hand in his. He stepped up to her, put an arm around her waist and pulled her close to him. She was surprised to find her heart racing, as she put her other hand on his shoulder.

They moved together for a while, to the soft tunes of the song. Ayesha soon found herself relaxing again and rested her head on his shoulder. Her long black hair waved to the rhythm of their movements.

Parth whispered into her ear, "Have I ever told you that I love it when you leave your hair open?"

Abashed, she just hid her face further into his chest.

When the song ended, the moment passed away, and they separated.

"You're a good dancer," Ayesha credited him.

"Not as good as you. You really seem to feel the music."

"I love dancing, but it's always nicer to have a good partner to dance with," she added.

"Mm... that's true. I discovered that today."

Ayesha watched him as he went and sat on the ledge by his window, looking down on 'his resort'. She was growing very fond of him. She could not help wonder sometimes though, as to how much of their friendship was purely innocent.

Was it all right to be with a boy in his room past midnight, even though they both knew they were not doing anything wrong? She wondered what Naina knew about their friendship.

"Parth...?" she asked as she plonked on his bed and took the pillow on her lap.

"Mm..."

"Does Naina know about me?"

"Yup."

"What does she know?"

"You're my neighbor."

"And...?"

"And what?" he asked.

"What else does she know?"

"Well, she doesn't need to know that Ayesha comes and sleeps every night in Parth's room," he teased.

Ayesha blushed furiously and looked down at the patterns on his bed-sheet. She didn't know what to say. Put like that, it sounded so wrong!

Perhaps, he was right in not telling Naina all the details. She won't understand. Ayesha herself hadn't enlightened Kavita on every single aspect of her time spent with Parth for the same reason. To someone sitting elsewhere, it couldn't sound perfectly usual.

But then, was their friendship perfectly usual at all?

Discomforted, Ayesha got up from the bed.

"Parth, let's go back on the terrace?"

"Hey! I wasn't serious. It's not so bad, you know. You've only slept with me for one night," he couldn't resist teasing her some more.

"Parth!!!," Ayesha exclaimed in exasperation. "C'mon."

"Okay, okay, we'll head back if you really want that."

They strolled under the stars for a while, talking about anything and everything: his days in UK, Kavita and Vikrant, her boss, Ahmedabad, Delhi.

"So when will you return to Ahmedabad next?" Parth posed the question that was on both of their minds.

"Till when are you here Parth?"

"End of June."

"And where will you be after that?"

"I have no clue where I will be transferred me."

"Your company has an office in Delhi?" she asked.

"Hmm..." Parth mumbled while glancing at his watch.

Ayesha had noticed this obsessive habit of his, over the last few days. He wore a huge watch on his wrist and had a custom of looking at it every now and then.

Exasperated, she finally asked, "Are you in a hurry Parth?"

He looked surprised as he replied, "No, why do you ask?"

"You're always glancing at your watch!"

"Oh! Is it? I didn't even realise I do that."

"Well, it comes across to the other person that you're in a hurry."

"It's just a meaningless habit. Don't get upset."

"Ok. By the way, what is the time?"

"So you are the one in a hurry," he taunted with an accusing expression.

Ayesha laughed at how naughty he could be!

"Tell me Parth! I have to wake up early again tomorrow. I think once I return to Delhi, I'll just be catching up on sleep for the first few days."

"Its 3:20."

"Oh my god!" she exclaimed. "I swear Parth, when I'm

with you, time just flies!!"

"Mm, I totally agree."

"I should probably head back now."

"Do you want to?"

"I don't want to Parth," she sighed. "I really like being with you, but I'm human and if I have to inhabit your world as well as the one my parents live in, I will need a few hours' sleep to survive."

"Ok, I'll drop you off then," he said, nodding in the direction of her room.

"Why don't I ever get to drop you off?" the thought suddenly dawned on her.

"Because... I can't allow a pretty young girl like you to go back on her own at this time of the night."

"I'll be fine Parth!" she laughed, "I would have been walking here even if I hadn't met you."

"But now you're my responsibility," he said righteously, holding her by the arm and steering her home-wards.

She gave in, but not without a warning, "One day I'll drop you off, ok?"

"We'll see."

"Uff! Stubborn boy!"

As they were nearing her room, she wondered if he would come and tuck her in again. She had really liked being pampered like that the previous night. However, he stopped just outside her door. She turned and stood facing him.

"Sleep well," he murmured.

"Goodnight Parth," she said, reluctant to let him go.

He smiled at her, touched her cheek and said, "Goodnight Ayesha."

chapter

8

Thursday morning dawned on Ayesha, leaving her with a saddening thought- she only had two more days here in Ahmedabad. She was flying back to Delhi on Sunday.

Somehow, more than despair at leaving home or returning to work, she grieved at the thought of leaving Parth behind.

All other thoughts were driven away from her mind when her Mother declared during lunch that a certain Mr and Mrs Kaushal would be coming home the next day with their son, to see Ayesha. It was a happy co-incidence, Savita assured her, that they were from Ahmedabad itself.

Ayesha was horrified at the thought, but really didn't know what to say to her mother. She felt too unprepared to face something like this the very next day!

Savita Khanna went on, "The boy works for Yes Bank here in Ahmedabad itself. He is a Manager at the bank. There is a lot of scope of growth in this sector, you know. He has studied in Bombay earlier. That is where Mr Kaushal was working. Now they are settled here only. Ayesha will be close to us if we do manage to find a boy in Ahmedabad."

The last few words were said looking directly at Col Khanna. Realising that a response was expected of him, he looked up briefly from his plate and nodded.

"Ashu beta," Mrs Khanna continued, "what will you wear tomorrow? Are you carrying a good *saree*?"

"Ma, can't we do this some other time? I'm not up to it."

"When else, child? You'll return to Delhi and then God only knows when you'll visit next. In any case you're going to meet Anant and Saurabh in Delhi. You might as well see this boy too, so that you can compare and think about it.

No one's compelling you to make an immediate decision. Just meet the boy."

Ayesha searched frantically in her mind for a good excuse, but her Mother had made it sound so simple that she couldn't think of an easy way out.

That evening they headed to the market to buy Ayesha appropriate clothes for the next day. The *saree* was chosen and purchased and the blouse was given to a tailor to stitch by next morning on a special urgent-order request.

Savita also pulled out some of her own jewelry to match with Ayesha's outfit. Handing them over to her daughter, just before they turned in for the night, her mother cautioned her.

"Do sleep in time Ashu. You've been looking very tired lately. We don't want you to look weary tomorrow. They'll be here by 11. Just give me a hand with the lay-out before you get dressed. And yes, Papa will bring your blouse from the tailor in the morning itself. Goodnight."

"Goodnight Ma," Ayesha rejoined in a deflated voice.

She headed upstairs, desperately wanting to unload all her troubles onto Parth. She placed the jewelry with the *saree*, put a pair of sandals next to them and looked around the room wondering if there was anything else she had to put in order for the next day.

~~❖~~

After brushing her teeth and washing her face, Ayesha headed out to the terrace and found Parth already there.

He was lying down on the ledge on his back and staring up at the stars. She went and sat down close to his head, peeked over into his eyes and waved her hand at him.

He smiled back.

Silence prevailed for a while. That was one of things Ayesha loved about being with Parth. They could share silences without getting uncomfortable or awkward.

Ayesha contemplated the next day. She tried to imagine the conventional scene of her walking into the drawing room with tea and snacks while the boy (what was his name?) and his parents evaluated her. She shuddered at the thought.

If only she could find herself a good boy on her own...

It was not like her parents were insisting on an arranged marriage. Her father had clearly asked her a couple of times if there was someone she would like them to meet. With all her prior relationships ending in disaster and with no faith in the possibility of her finding someone suitable, she had not stopped them from beginning the search themselves.

She sighed.

"You seem to have heavy thoughts on your mind today," Parth commented.

"A boy is coming to see me tomorrow."

Parth raised his eyebrows. "For marriage?"

"No! Just to say Hi!" she said sarcastically. "Of course Parth! What else?"

Sensing her anxiety, he sat up and put an arm around her.

She slumped against him, with her head resting on his shoulder.

"You don't want to get married?" he asked gently.

"It's not that Parth. I don't know. I don't feel ready yet... I'm scared," she added as an afterthought.

He stroked her arm lightly, waiting for her to go on.

"I'm so confused Parth. I do know that I have to get married eventually. There's no harm starting to look out now either, because it will give me time to get to know the guy before we get married. But I just feel scared. I've misjudged men in my life too many times now. I've always ended up with the wrong guy. I'm terrified that I'll end up with the wrong guy again... and this time we'll be married."

A tear trickled down her face. Parth felt fiercely protective towards her. He wished he could do something, but he knew this was a terrain where he just couldn't step in.

After much thought, he finally said, "Ayesha... Baby, you'll have to go out there and try. You may fall down. Get up, dust yourself and try again. I know it's tougher than it sounds. Would it help if I say that I'm there for you? If any guy troubles you ever again, just let me know and I'll come to Delhi and bash him up, ok?"

She smiled, looked up at him and said, "Thank you Parth. It does feel nice to know that somehow."

They sat there for a while, her head leaning against his shoulder, his arm wrapped protectively around her. She felt safe sitting there with him, but she knew that someday she would have to step out into the world on her own and make an attempt again. She only wasn't sure if she was ready for it yet.

In an attempt to cheer her up, Parth asked, "So are you dressing up traditionally tomorrow?"

"Yes, I'll be wearing a *saree.* We went to buy one today because I wasn't carrying any of my *sarees* here."

"Mm... *Sarees* are very sexy."

Ayesha sat up straight and laughed, "Ahh! Now I remember seeing that in your sketch!"

He just smiled.

"So why exactly do you find a *saree* sexy?" Ayesha asked with a wink.

"Mm... It hides some... and reveals some... at the right places."

"Aha! The right places! And what are these 'right places'?" she asked in delight.

"I've already told you too much! I'm not saying anything more!"

"No, please do. There are no secrets between us. C'mon!"

"Mm... Maybe I'll show you tomorrow," he said with a twinkle in his eye.

Ayesha blushed! She had no retort.

He smiled, noticing her bashfulness, and continued in the same tone, "So how are you tying it?"

"How am I tying it?" Ayesha asked, confused by the question.

"Mm... There are three ways of tying a *saree*: one is very decent, with everything covered up; the second is 'sexy', showing just the right amount of 'the right places'; and the third is slutty."

"Ahh... I see. And which way should I tie my *saree*?" she asked with an innocent expression.

"Mm... So call me once you've worn your *saree* tomorrow, and I'll give it the finishing touches. I'll just touch and feel..." Parth paused here to watch Ayesha blush again and then continued, "...the *saree* and check that everything's all right, ok?"

She laughed at his daring and assured him she would let him 'check her out'. She however, had no such real intention, and both of them knew it.

She got up from the ledge, stretched herself and asked, "Let's take a walk?"

They strolled around on her terrace for a while.

"Parth," Ayesha said in between, "I'm here only for one more night. Then I return to Delhi. Will you stay in touch?"

"Do you want me to?"

"Yes"

"Then I will."

"Do you want to?"

"Mm... I do."

Ayesha mulled over this for a while, then said, "You know Parth, with you I feel like I've found a 'forever' kind of friend. We may or may not talk regularly. But whenever we will talk or meet, I feel like we would be as if we never parted. I feel really comfortable with you."

"Mm... It's actually quite incredible, the way we've grown close to each other, the way I can tell you things I've never told anyone before."

"I like listening to you, you know. When you talk about your college days, there is a happy look on your face."

"That's true. Talking to you has made me recollect a lot of the good times. Thank you for that," he said with a fond smile.

"You don't have to thank me. I actually like the fact that with you, I'm more of a listener than a talker."

"So that makes us a fine combination," he declared.

"Totally!" she agreed. "That's what is best about being with you. When I feel like talking, I find a good listener in you. And when I just feel like distracting myself and unwinding, I like sitting back and listening to you talk."

Around 2am in the night, Ayesha decided to tuck in for the night. Her Mom was expecting her down early the next morning to help with putting the house in order and preparing for the guests. She would also need an hour to get ready, tie the *saree* and dress up.

Parth let her go on the promise that she would call him to 'help' her with the *saree*-draping. "I will wake up and be waiting, all right?"

"We'll see!" she said at her door-step. "Goodnight Parth."

He replied with a smile, "Goodnight Ayesha."

~~❖~~

The morning brought with it a flurry of activity. Col Khanna pushed off to visit the tailor, pick up some hot *samosas* and sweets.

Savita Khanna took over the kitchen and its responsibilities, while Ayesha devoted herself to tidying up the drawing room. The drawing room was a good reflection of the Army-life they had led, with its varied collection of souvenirs from different parts of the country.

Once things were in a modicum of order, Savita dispatched Ayesha upstairs to take her time and get ready. There was still an hour and a half before the Kaushals dropped in.

After a bath, Ayesha just sat on her bed in a bath-robe for a while, anticipating the events later in the morning. She reached for her phone to message Parth, but then felt that he would be asleep and so gave up on the idea.

She got up and got dressed. While draping the *saree*, she remembered Parth's theory on 'three ways of tying a *saree*' and smiled. Just then her phone rang. It was an unknown number.

"Hello," she said.

"Ayesha..."

She froze. She could not be mistaken. This was Shiven.

Why was he calling her now? It had been over a year since they had broken up. He had called once in between, but Tushar had been around then. He had spoken directly to Shiven and asked him to leave Ayesha alone.

"Ayesha... How are you?" he tried again.

"Why are you calling Shiven?"

"I just wanted to speak to you once."

"About what?"

"I want you to believe me Ayesha, I never cheated on you. She liked me, but I didn't respond."

"Shiven, I don't need this now. In any case, it doesn't matter. I've moved on."

"It matters to me!" he raised his voice.

"Shiven, please!"

"What please? You just cut yourself off from me. You never even gave me a chance to justify. Ayesha, I still think about you. But you've found yourself some other guy, it seems. Tell him to speak to me directly. I'll tell him to buzz off. Who is he to keep you away from me? Does he know how much you love me?"

Ayesha didn't know how to respond! What was she supposed to say to this?

"Shiven, please don't call me after this. I have moved on. Please let me get on with my life. Bye."

She cut the call abruptly, but the memories came flooding

back in. She had loved him so much and he had been with someone else all along. She had given him everything he wanted. Except one thing. And he'd gone and found himself another girl for that. Tears dropped down her eyes at the thought of the humiliation she had undergone in his hands.

She started, when the phone rang again. She looked at it anxiously, but was relieved to see it was Parth.

"Hello," she said in a small voice.

"Ayesha."

She started crying on the phone. How she wished Shiven hadn't called now. All those things she had been trying to forget were coming back to her mind in a rush.

"I'll be there in a minute," Parth said urgently.

When Ayesha didn't stop him, he cut the call and hopped across. He was in her room in less than a minute. He quickly latched the door leading to the rest of the house, lest her mother drop in and find him there! He then went and sat beside Ayesha.

"What happened, girl?"

Ayesha didn't know what to say. There was too much to tell. She just wept. Parth put his arms around her and let her cry for some time. He glanced at his watch. 10:20am.

"Is the boy still coming to see you?" he asked.

She nodded into his chest. He could feel his t-shirt going wet with the tears. This wouldn't do. All this crying, it would show on her face. He slowly moved her face away from his chest and tried to wipe her tears away.

"Ayesha... Baby, you'll have to be strong. C'mon, you can't sit here and cry, you have to get ready."

She looked at the watch too, and realised he was right.

She sat up and wiped her face. Then got up and went to the bathroom.

Once she had washed and wiped her face, she came back to Parth and asked, “Does it look like I’ve been crying?”

“Well, apart from the tomato-coloured nose, not really.”

Ayesha laughed a little and hurried to the mirror.

“But you look quite sexy in the *saree*,” he remarked, trying to humour her.

She smiled nervously, while trying to hide all signs of her weeping with make-up. She then combed out her long black hair and held it together at the back with a clip. Just when she was looking at herself in the full-length mirror, she saw Parth come up behind her. Through the mirror, she saw him undo the clip and shake out her hair.

“You look better this way,” Parth murmured.

“So, am I all set to go?” she asked.

Still standing behind her, he looked at her reflection from top to toe. Draped in a red *saree* that flattered her curves, Ayesha looked elegant and pretty. She wore small gold drops in her ears and a few red and gold bangles.

“You look gorgeous.”

She turned around and smiled.

“Thanks Parth.”

“Thanks for what?”

“For being there...”

chapter

9

Ayesha couldn't help wondering if this was for real. She was sitting amidst her parents and the Kaushals, telling them about her hobbies, and thinking to herself, "My hobbies are going to decide if I'll make a good wife to their son?!"

The boy, Ujjwal, was mostly quiet, unless he was prodded to say something. When they were finally left alone in the garden in front of Ayesha's house to 'get to know each other better', neither of them seemed to know what to say.

After a long pause, Ujjwal finally said, "Frankly, I need to tell you this. I'm not interested in getting married."

Noticing her startled expression, he quickly clarified, "Please don't take me amiss. You're a very nice girl. It's just that I'm in the very early stages of my career and I can't afford to take on added responsibilities of marriage right now."

Ayesha couldn't help but grin broadly and say, "Well, that's all right. I'm not in a particular hurry myself."

He looked relieved. He pointed at the swings in the garden and asked, "Shall we sit?"

"Yeah, sure."

Once they had sat on adjacent swings, he looked curious. "So if you're not interested either, why are your parents looking around?"

"You know how it is in our society, right? It's been a year since I graduated and have been working. My parents feel that they should start looking around, so that in a year or two, I'd be able to settle down."

"Ok, time-wise that would suit me actually. I'd probably be ready to get married by then."

Ayesha began feeling apprehensive again. Was he saying he'd like to get married to her after two years then?

He continued, "But again, to be honest, there is another girl I like. I'm not sure if anything will come of it, but I do want to give it a try."

Ayesha began smiling to herself. Awesome!

So he wasn't interested in marriage, and even if he was, it was with another girl! How she wished the two Delhi guys turned out to have similar stories.

~~❖~~

Ayesha and Parth were laughing together. She had just narrated the incidents of the morning to him.

"O God! He totally broke your heart," Parth declared in mock-sympathy.

"He sure did! I was almost in tears!"

"Which reminds me, what happened to you today morning? Why were you so upset?" he ventured.

Ayesha went quiet. She didn't know what to say. She was lying down on the ledge between their terraces, with her head in his lap.

"Someone called. Someone from my past."

He waited, to see if she would add anything to that. She didn't. Sensing that she did not want to talk about it, he didn't enquire any further.

They sat in silence, she contemplating why Shiven had called out of the blue; he pondering over this dark past of hers that she never spoke about.

When quiet had prevailed for far too long, Parth, missing her usual chatter, finally said, "You're in another world today."

A sad smile spread on her face as she looked up at him

from where her head lay on his lap.

"Come back to me," he said, softly. "You realise that after today, we only have one more night together, right?"

"I've been trying not to think about it," she replied. "I'll miss you, Parth."

"I'll miss you too," he said, as he gently stroked her hair.

Ayesha felt a drop on her forehead. She looked up to check if Parth was crying!

He was looking up at the sky. "I think it's drizzling," Parth exclaimed, even as more drops began to fall. Ayesha sat up.

"What now?" she asked urgently. They couldn't possibly get wet in the middle of the night.

"C'mon!" he said as he swung on to his side of the terrace. The rain was a steady pour by now. He took her hand and raced towards the staircase in his house.

They were laughing by the time they reached. The rain had managed to make them fairly damp. They stepped down into his room still giggling at this sudden adventure. Parth took out a towel and handed it to Ayesha, who wiped her hair and face with it.

Just as she was about to settle onto his couch again, she heard him call her. When she turned around, she saw Parth standing with an umbrella at the door that led into the rest of the house!

"Where are we going?" she asked in surprise.

"You ask too many questions."

Amused, Ayesha followed him out of his room and down a set of stairs to the drawing room of the house.

"Aren't your parents at home?" she whispered.

"Mm... They are."

"Then what are we doing here? How will you explain my presence if they turn up suddenly?" she continued in a soft tone, but this time sounding far more panicky.

Parth, who was leading the way stopped, turned back at her and smiled. He then took her hand in his and continued to walk across the drawing room to a door on the other side.

Her heart beating fast, Ayesha followed obediently, trusting him. She looked around at the splendor of the room in admiration. It was expensively done up and in good taste.

When they reached the door, Parth slipped the latch open, and still holding onto Ayesha's hand stepped out. They were, Ayesha realised, at the side-garden of the house. On the right, a path led to the front garden which she had seen from the roof. On the left, a path led to a pretty gazebo surrounded by flowers.

When Parth opened the umbrella and pulled her under it, she realised they were headed for the hexagonal shaped gazebo. Covered from the top with a sloping roof, the gazebo was open on all other sides. When they reached their destination, he shook out the umbrella, put it in one corner to dry and came and stood beside Ayesha.

She was standing to one side, looking out and realising why he had brought her all the way here. With the rain-water sliding off the sloping roof, water was pouring down all sides of the structure. It was like looking out onto the world from behind a wall of water, and the world sure looked pretty from there. She smiled in pleasure.

"Do you like it?" he asked, in a soft voice.

"Like it? I love it Parth. It's beautiful!"

"I always come here when it rains, especially in the night."

Suddenly reminded of ground realities, Ayesha asked, "What if your parents see us here?"

"It's a risk worth taking to experience this. I don't think they will wake up and come out. They know I come here sometimes at night, so even if they heard something, they would know it's me."

"Hmm," she was not completely convinced, but decided to take a chance. After all, this wasn't the first time they were doing something crazy. She turned towards her partner-in-crime and realised he had been watching her.

He took a step back towards the center of the gazebo and offered his hand to her. She tilted her head to one side, took his hand and he pulled her close to him. Parth raised her left hand to his shoulder, put his hand around her waist and held her other hand in his. Softly, to the rhythm of the rain, they danced together.

Ayesha looked up into his eyes and saw Parth looking straight into hers. The beat of her heart quickened. Their eyes locked, their faces close to each other, their arms around one another- Parth and Ayesha swayed.

What was this, she wondered. Where does the line of friendship end, and where do we cross it? She wasn't sure, nor did she want to know just then. All she knew was that it was a beautiful moment, just the two of them, dancing slowly with the rain pattering down all around.

chapter

10

Ayesha woke up early on Saturday and lay in bed thinking about Parth. She had known him for six days, but felt like she'd known him forever. She re-lived the previous night in her thoughts. Her heart beat fast again when she recollected the way they had danced together in the rain, so close to each other.

She couldn't deny that at times she felt strongly attracted to him. Till where could she explain it away as friendship? Was she doing something wrong? She thought of Naina and felt uncomfortable.

But when she thought of Parth again and the moments spent with him this last week, all other thoughts receded to the back of her mind and she simply felt happy.

She remembered that first night and the way she had initially felt enraged at his audacity. She thought of the crazy drive on the highway, the night she slept off on his couch, the way he had carried her like a baby and tucked her into bed, his room and his sketches, the way he had consoled her after Shiven called. She smiled when she recollected their conversation about the *saree*. And she thought again of the previous night.

Parth... She thought of him and dozed off again.

~~❖~~

The day was spent preparing for her return to Delhi.

Together, mother and daughter prepared snacks and food items that Ayesha would carry back with her. Ayesha also spent time with her father. They usually did not talk much, yet shared a strong bonding. They played Scrabble together, and she talked about her work.

Later in the evening, the family went out for dinner. Not knowing when they would see their only daughter again, the Khannas were inclined to pamper her that day.

Ayesha's thoughts frequently escaped to the house next door and the dimly-lit room upstairs. She was slightly agitated by the thought that after this night, she may never see Parth again. He would be transferred elsewhere and in a country as big as ours, she thought, we could easily be lost to each other.

They would keep in touch, no doubt, but things were never the same after one parted ways. The phone could never be a perfect substitute for a good friend's physical presence. No one knew this better than Ayesha, who had made numerous attempts to preserve her most precious friendships during the Army years, but gradually grew distanced from all her close friends, as she and they found new people in the new cities they moved to.

"Ashu," her mother interrupted her thoughts, as they sat together in front of the TV that night.

"Yes Ma?" Ayesha asked sweetly, being in a mood to oblige her parents.

"Keep this carefully," her mother handed her an envelope. "It has the contact details of both the boys, Anant and Saurabh. I have also written the tentative time of meeting that I fixed with their parents. You can, however, call them personally and fix up a time that is mutually convenient."

Ayesha nodded.

"Do keep me updated about the meetings and what comes of them. I'll proceed in talks with the parents accordingly.

And child, don't feel pressurised at all. No one's forcing you into anything. But one of these boys might just turn out to be a suitable boy for you. Meet them with an open mind."

Ayesha nodded again.

Col Khanna added from his side, "I hope you enjoyed your stay here. Do come over again whenever you find time. Ahmedabad is not very far from Delhi. Drop in whenever you feel like. Remember, this is your home."

Once back in her room, Ayesha packed her bags, checked and double-checked the room, bathroom and cupboards to ensure she hadn't left anything behind. Her flight was early in the morning and she didn't want to leave anything for the last minute. She set aside her journey clothes and then stepped out into the fresh air.

It had rained during the day as well, and there was a slight chill in the air. The breeze was fresh and there was the smell of wet earth in the air. Ayesha sighed in pleasure and began strolling. Parth was not in sight, but she was sure he would come soon.

~~❖~~

"Tell me something Parth."

"Mm...?"

"What do you think about marriage?"

"My marriage?"

"Yes."

"I'm scared too."

"You are? Have you decided when you're settling down?"

"Naina is my age. I can wait another year, two at max.

There is already talk at home about when to plan the wedding."

"Your mother knows about Naina?"

"Yup! She's known all along. She knows Naina's parents quite well. They were friends from before. She's happy."

"Hmm... So have you never ever had another girl in your life? Have you ever thought about someone else?"

Parth looked thoughtful.

"When I was in UK," he said slowly, "a German girl came on exchange for a year... This was about 3 years back... I had signed up as a buddy for incoming exchange students and I was assigned to help her settle in. We spent a lot of time together initially, while I showed her around the city and helped her feel at home... Caro... Caroline actually, but I called her Caro."

He paused. Ayesha didn't want to butt in, so she made no comment and waited for him to continue. She had noticed over the last few days that one of the best ways to get Parth to open up and talk was to stay silent herself.

"I had mentioned Naina to her some time. So she knew. Just before returning to her country, she had told me that if ever I have reason to think beyond Naina, she would be waiting for me. I kind of knew all along that she liked me. So I was not surprised."

Another long pause as he seemed to collect his thoughts.

"But I was amazed when she called me a few days back to say she was coming to India and would like to meet me."

"She's coming to Ahmedabad?!"

"I don't know yet. She said she was yet to finalise her itinerary. She's coming towards the end of this month."

Ayesha wondered whether to ask the question; then

decided to go ahead. “Did you like her too?”

“Mm... I liked her... But I don’t think I loved her.”

“So have you ever met anyone who made you think twice about Naina?”

“Mm...” he said after a short pause.

“Caroline?”

“No.”

“Someone else?” she enquired further. Intrigued, she sat up straight and turned to face him.

“I have been thinking lately,” he replied, “as to what it would have been like... if I was single when I had met you...”

Ayesha blinked. What could she say to this? She had herself had this thought a couple of times. What if Parth had been single when they had met? She really did like him. That he was fond of her, seemed rather obvious as well. After spending so much time together, things could have easily moved ahead. Would she have wanted that?

Brooding on similar lines, he turned and looked straight into her eyes, to judge her reaction. Confused, Ayesha looked down at her hands in her lap and said, “I’ve thought about it too.”

“Would you have been interested, Ayesha?”

She was in a fix. This was awkward. Would she have been interested? She was so suspicious of love and relationships that she was always fighting back anyone who seemed to approach her with that intention.

Knowing that Parth was committed was a big reason behind why she had allowed herself to grow close to him. If he had been single, she wondered if she would have spent as much time with him. She would have been too afraid of falling into emotional entanglements.

But now? Now that she knew him and liked him? Could she see herself with Parth? But why was she even thinking about all this? What about Naina? Why was he asking her such questions now? What was the point of thinking on those lines?

She looked up at him in bewilderment. He seemed to be waiting for an answer.

Would I have been interested?

"I like you, Parth. Time just flies when I'm with you. I like the way we can talk about anything and everything. I like the way we can share thoughts, and even share silences. I like being with you. I haven't thought of anything beyond that."

"Today morning when you were crying and I was holding you close to me," he said softly, looking far off into the sky, "I didn't want to let you go. I want to be able to take care of you... always. Your tears make me sad and I feel elated when I can bring a smile on your face... You've brightened up my life Ayesha. It makes me so unbelievably happy to just be with you."

Ayesha was dazed.

Was Parth saying all this purely as a friend? She felt torn. Here was a boy she loved being with, who was telling her he wanted to be with her and care for her forever.

He understood her so well. He was there when she needed him. He was romantic in his own sweet way. They could laugh together on the silliest of things; they could sit together in companionable silence for hours. Every time she was anxious or joyful, she sought him out to share her feelings with.

Wasn't this what she was looking for in her search for love?

Yet the thought of Naina continued to loom in her head. Ayesha looked at Parth, who was sitting beside her, looking pensive. Without looking at her, he just put his hand on hers, which lay on the ledge between them. She didn't pull back. They sat that way for a long time, each trying to sort out the muddle of thoughts in their heads.

They had already said enough, and neither had the courage to broach the issue any further. It is never easy to ruffle feathers. Naina existed and that was a reality they could not evade. Yet, Ayesha and Parth were a reality too. What they shared between them was difficult to put a name to; friendship, but bordering on something more, something magical.

After all, do six-day old friends feel the pain of an impending separation so acutely? Do they ask themselves over and over again as to when they will meet again? Do all the special moments of the past few days keep flooding back in their waking hours?

What was this spark, this magic between them? Something neither of them had ever experienced before.

~~❖~~

"I think I should head back now," Ayesha said after a while.

It was close to 3 am. She had to wake up in 3 hours!

"I don't want to let you go," Parth said firmly. His hand still lay on hers.

Ayesha looked into his eyes in anguish. She wanted to throw her arms around him and say, I don't want to go either Parth! I don't want to go anywhere away from you. The thought of not being able to see you every night kills me.

Who will hold me when I cry the next time? Who will tease me? Who will care for me? Who will I share my life with?

She didn't say any of this.

But her eyes said it all.

Parth got off the ledge and came and stood in front of her, while she continued to sit. He framed her face with his hands and when he could not stand the agony in her eyes any longer, he put his arms around her and held her close to him.

Ayesha rested her heavy heart against Parth and let him hold her. Slowly, tears of helplessness began to flow down her face. Parth put a finger under her chin and raised her head. At the sight of her distress, he wiped her tears away and kissed her forehead.

"Baby..." Parth whispered softly into her ears. "I'll always be there for you. No matter what, no matter where I go and where you live. No matter whom I marry and who you settle with. Remember that you'll always hold a special place in my heart. If ever you need me, you just have to reach out and I'll be there. Ok?"

Ayesha began sobbing louder. She felt she was losing him. She held him tight, unwilling to let the moment end.

What if she never saw him again?

What if this was the end?

Gradually, when her weeping reduced, Parth pulled her away from him and wiped her face again.

"Shhh," he whispered.

He gave her his hand. She understood. This was it. This was the end. The final walk.

She put her hand in his one last time and got off the ledge.

They walked towards her door, hand-in-hand, but without a word on their lips.

Parth squeezed her hand in a wordless goodbye.

He had already said a lot... and left a lot unsaid. It had to remain that way.

He had to let it remain that way... He had to let her go.

chapter 11

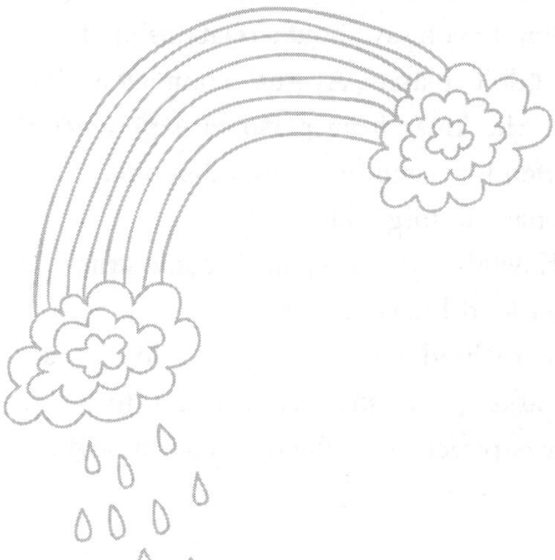

The crowd around the canal had thinned out as it was beginning to get late. Ayesha turned to look at Parth. He looked almost the same- suave, confident, sincere. She wondered what had happened of his life since then. The days after she had left him and Ahmedabad had been painful for her.

She had realised, with increasing conviction that she had fallen in love. However, knowing well that he was committed, to be married, she had pushed him away.

She thought back to those agonising months, that had followed.

~~❖~~

"Ashu, I know you. You have a broken heart!"

"No Ka, how can I? I hardly knew him for a week. One doesn't fall in love so fast?"

"Can you say with 100% conviction that you haven't lost your heart to him?" Kavita pressed on.

Ayesha, sitting on a beanbag in her balcony, sighed. She had no answer. Kavita too, didn't know what to say to her friend. What do you say about a relationship that cannot exist?

She didn't blame Ayesha completely for what had happened. She knew from personal experience that the line between friendship and love was a thin one.

"You have to forget him."

"No Kavita!" Ayesha rejoined, panic-struck. "I don't want to lose the friend I have in him."

Kavita realised this wasn't going to be easy. In a soft voice she asked, "Ayesha, can you talk to him every night, share your experiences of the day, your thoughts and feelings and yet, not grow closer to him? Can you sleep with a clear conscience knowing that Naina is unaware that Parth speaks to you every night? Can you totally erase from your mind those feelings of attraction you have felt for him?"

Ayesha had contemplated these questions herself, but had tried to ignore the answers because she didn't want to know them. It had been a week since she had returned from Ahmedabad.

When she had found herself messaging Parth multiple times in the day and realised that her mind was with him almost all day, she had called Kavita, knowing that she needed some sane advice.

When all her questions met silence, Kavita knew that she had struck home.

"Think about it Ayesha. Don't kid yourself. What you both share is more than just friendship. That he is committed in another relationship is a fact that you both have got to accept. Keeping in touch is not the best way to get over him. Do this soon and do it fast. The more you delay, the more pain it is going to bring to all the people involved."

Even after Kavita had hung up, Ayesha sat in her balcony brooding for a long time.

She glanced at the clock hanging inside the room. 10:30pm. Parth would be about to call her. They had been speaking to each other every night since she had returned from Ahmedabad. Animated conversations dwindled into sweet nothings until she fell asleep, with him still murmuring to her on the phone. If she was to take Kavita's advice, she needed to put an end to this habit of theirs. What would she tell Parth?

The irony of the situation struck Ayesha suddenly. Hadn't she been searching for love? Was she now running away from it? Why had she had to have gone and found love in the most difficult of places? Had she even known that they were heading this way?

Was she a fool to have imagined that all those midnight rendezvous were absolutely innocent and platonic? Or were they? What would two friends do? Won't they also meet and talk? What made this different then? She couldn't put her finger to it, but her gut feeling told her they had crossed the line somewhere.

'When?', was a million dollar question.

The ring of the cell phone lying beside her shattered her thoughts.

'Parth calling'

The very sight of those words filled her with elation. How could she close the door to such happiness? Did she really need to? Couldn't she retain the friend she had in him?

"Hi Parth"

"Ayesha..."

"I was just thinking about you," she said softly.

"Mm... And what were you thinking?"

Tough question. How was she to answer that? Her hesitation told him there was a problem at hand.

"What happened, girl? Tell me..."

"Parth... where do you think we're headed?"

Silence. He knew where this conversation was going.

Ayesha felt disappointed. She didn't know why, though. What answer was she expecting? She took a deep breath and decided to take the plunge.

"Parth, what you and I share is more than friendship. You realise that, right?"

"What are you trying to say?"

Her shoulders slumped. He was being evasive.

"What I'm saying is that... Parth, please try and understand me. We have grown very close in the last ten days. More than what might be acceptable to Naina. If we go on like this, there will come a day when probably Naina will get to know and you will have to completely let go off me. Else, my own conscience will ensure the same. Either way we will lose each other. I don't want that Parth. I treasure your friendship. I want to retain that. And to do that, we have to limit ourselves to only friendship. You understand what I'm saying?"

Ayesha's words met with silence. For a moment, her heart skipped a beat. She had been very frank and put in words what they both knew but had never acknowledged. What if he denied it all?

"Mm..." finally he uttered. "Ok."

"That's all?" she asked in exasperation. Had he nothing else to say?

"You're right Ayesha," he said slowly, as if the words were weighing him down. "We've been fooling ourselves. But I don't want to lose you. Are you going away from me?"

He sounded like a child, who was about to lose his precious toy. Ayesha's heart went out to him. She could understand his anxiety. She, too, shared it.

If she had been lonely and had found a friend in Parth, he too, hadn't known a friend this intimately. Naina and he loved each other, but they had never been physically proximate. The kind of intimate time and personal conversations Ayesha and Parth had shared in the last few days was probably a novel experience for him too.

"I don't want to lose you either Parth. That is why I'm saying all this. I'm not going anywhere. But we need to be more conscious of our interactions. Please be my friend."

Neither knew what exactly they meant by this. Where had that nebulous line been when they had stepped beyond the boundary of the platonic? What were they supposed to change in their interactions? What exactly was 'acceptable' and within norms of pure friendship?

More importantly, was it possible to retreat and return to that sacred line of 'only friendship'? Or was it irreversible to the extent that it would only find cure in a complete break away?

~~❖~~

Eventually she had realised that they couldn't keep up the farce. As waves of guilt washed over her time and again, Ayesha had started withdrawing from Parth. She avoided replying to his messages, sometimes didn't return his calls. It had taken her all her will power to let him go.

"So did you find your Mr Right, finally?" Parth broke the silence.

She hesitated, then nodded.

Parth turned his eyes away and looked back at the canal. What had he expected? Of course she would have moved on. He had never given her a reason to wait for him.

It was only after she had left that he had realised what he had let go of.

God knew he had tried. He had called her incessantly when she stopped picking up his calls. He had texted her and emailed her. But he could promise her nothing. As she continued to go into a shell, he had eventually been struck with the thought that what he was doing to her was unfair.

He had to let her move on and settle. He could not offer her a life together and he could not expect her to wait infinitely. Moreover, wait for what?

With a broken heart, Parth had stayed away from Ayesha. They had never added each other on Facebook and had no common friends. Her parents had moved from Ahmedabad after a year, and his family didn't know where they had gone. As the years passed away, he often found himself wondering what had happened to her and how she was doing.

Ayesha stood up after some time. "I should leave. It's late."

Of course, her family would be waiting for her.

"May I walk you home?"

She was about to shake her head, then relented.

As they walked back slowly, Parth asked, "So what are you doing in Amsterdam? Do you live here?"

"No. I'm here on an assignment. I don't know if you remember, but I'm a travel-writer. I work for a UK-based firm now and travel across the world. I'm in Amsterdam for the next few weeks."

"Do you enjoy your work?" Parth asked, almost enviously, thinking back about the monotony of his desk-job."

"Hmm... yes, I do. It keeps me on the move. And there is so much beauty to be explored in this world. I feel like I could travel my entire life and yet not see everything I would like to!"

He had always admired her zest for life. As they rounded a

corner, Ayesha stopped under an apartment and said, "We've reached. I'll take your leave."

Parth suddenly felt desperate. He did not want to let her go and yet, what right did he have to hold her back? He blurted, "You married Anant?"

Ayesha looked confused for a moment. Then recollecting, she looked at him with a painful expression.

"No Parth... I never got married."

Tears glistened in her eyes, as she turned around and entered the building.

chapter

12

Parth was still reeling from what he had heard the last night. He was at work, but mentally elsewhere.

He kept replaying the moment in his head, trying to make sense of it. Why had she not married? All these years, he had pictured her married to Anant or another eligible groom chosen by her family. He had imagined that she had settled into a comfortable family life and possibly forgotten him. He had often mused that she would have made a great wife and mother.

He suddenly felt frustrated about why he hadn't taken her phone number. He wanted to reach out to her. He wasn't yet sure if she wanted to speak to him, but she hadn't resisted yesterday. Moreover, now that he had found her after so long, he couldn't let her go as easily. Not this time.

Parth switched tabs on his computer and Googled her name - something he had stopped himself from doing all these years. A number of search results showed up- Ayesha Khanna, travel-writer, freelance writer, author. She had written a couple of books and had been recognised on several platforms.

He found a page that spoke about Ayesha's personal life.

A nomad by nature, Ayesha Khanna, has never rooted herself to a single city. The daughter of an Indian Army Officer, Ayesha spent her early childhood traversing the length and breadth of India. From cantonments on the outskirts of little towns to defense settlements in some larger cities, she remained on the move.

Ayesha started her career with Rolling Stones, a Delhi-based travel and tourism company. As her work won accolades, Ayesha started freelancing for many big-ticket Travel Magazines and companies. Today, her travel takes her across the continents as she continues to pursue her passion in writing and traveling. In her spare time, she also teaches Tourism courses as a guest lecturer in London, Amsterdam and Milan.

No mention of a family or children. Nor did any of the other pages throw further light on this aspect of her life.

Parth was intrigued.

~~❖~~

Try as she might, Ayesha was unable to focus on anything. Her inadequate preparation and lack of attention had made her bluster through most of the class today. The students must have noticed that. They were generous enough to let her get away with it.

Why had he come back into her life? It had taken her so long to get some sense of order back into her life. She had never gotten over him, but at least she had come to peace with the fact that he would have settled and would be forever, out of her reach now.

Sometimes she chided herself at the thought of how six days with someone had altered her life. How could she have fallen so completely in love in such a short while?

There were no simple answers, but then life never promises simple answers. All she knew was that she had not been able to settle for anyone else after that. Having always struggled to find love in her life, when she had finally chanced upon it, destiny had decided to put it out of her reach.

She could not possibly have married anyone else. It would have been unfair on the boy and on her. After all, it was injustice to live with someone and dream of someone else. In fact, it would have been most unjust to the children born out of such a farce of a marriage. She had never been able to explain these things to her parents.

For a while, they had persuaded her and pleaded with her. Eventually, they had left her alone. She often felt bad for them. She knew they craved to see her settled. They wanted to play with their grandchildren, like other people in their circles did.

She almost wished she had had a sibling who might have fulfilled their dreams. Despite all of this, however, she could not get herself to marry anyone.

As time had gone by, she had taken to her work with unrestrained passion. Her work was her life now. Her students, her readers, her publishers- they were her family.

Traveling and writing filled in those empty spaces in her life that would have otherwise been devoted to her own home and family. She loved her work, she loved seeing new places, she loved walking down alleys of a new town. The sense of freedom and independence it gave her were unmatched.

And then – Parth had walked straight back into her life, turning it all topsy-turvy.

She sighed and turned on her laptop. She had to prepare for her class the next day. She could not, would not allow him to disrupt everything she had so carefully built.

~~❖~~

As Ayesha stepped out of her apartment at 8.45am, heading to the college where she was teaching as a guest lecturer this term, she was startled to see Parth sitting on the pavement across the road. Since when had he been sitting there?

She had a mind to turn and walk away. Her heart did not let her. She walked across the road and sat down next to him.

"I didn't have your phone number," he said simply.

Ayesha turned to look him in the eye. "Why do you want my number, Parth?"

"I want to know how you are, Ayesha. How are you doing? Is everything all right in your life? You remember I had once vowed to be there for you. You chose to move away and I let you. But I still care very deeply for you."

She didn't know what to say. He was saying all the things she craved to hear from him. But it wasn't right. He was a married man, committed to someone else. Guilt pricked her again. What if his wife knew that he had come out this morning to sit across a girl's house?

As if to remind him, she asked, "How's Naina?"

He gave her a curious look. "She is fine."

She wanted him to feel the same guilt she did. So she pestered further, "Do you have kids?"

Parth was quiet for a while. She wondered if she had touched upon something sensitive.

Finally, after a long time, he said, "Naina never married me. We are in touch. She lives in India. She married someone else."

Ayesha was stunned. Her mind surged with a million thoughts. Why had they not got married? She had given him up for Naina and they never got married? All these years of staying away, of persuading herself that he was happy and she should not disrupt his life. All those moments of guilt she suffered, feeling responsible towards Naina!

"W..why?" she stammered, still reeling with shock.

Parth looked down at his hands, then turned to look at her.

“I started working soon after you left. I was posted in a plant in a small town in Andhra Pradesh. The work was demanding and I would often spend most of the day and sometimes all night working there. I was not being able to give her the time and attention I should have. Gradually, it drove a wedge between us. She was willing to give up her career and join me, but she wanted to marry a man, not his house. I was hardly ever home.”

He went quiet. Ayesha gently put a hand on his shoulder, but he continued to stare down at the pavement. Finally, in a voice so soft, she could hardly hear it, he said,

“I screwed up... twice. With you and Naina. I’m so sorry...”

chapter

13

Ayesha had a week left in Amsterdam. Parth had pleaded with her to stay on for a while, but she had to reach London for a series of lectures she had promised to conduct. Moreover, she was not yet willing to give up everything she had built brick-by-brick for herself over the last few years.

They sat on a bench by one of the canals, hand-in-hand. Ayesha leaned her head on Parth's shoulder. She was puzzled at herself. She knew she had found happiness at last, but then why was she so scared to give herself to him. Was she afraid of being left in the lurch again? Of being left empty and alone? What was holding her back?

The last three weeks had been magical, no doubt. Time just flew by, when she was with Parth. They were like kids when they were together! He had shown her hidden parts of the city, which she would never have discovered on her own. They had climbed the roof of an official building in the night, slipping past a dozing guard. They had rented skates and practiced in Vondelpark, until Ayesha was sore with all the falls she had taken.

He had even taken her to the notorious 'red-light district', where she had looked on with amazement. The evening they had tried 'Space Cakes' at Hill Street Blues, Ayesha couldn't stop giggling until late into the night! Parth had finally had to hold her down on her bed, until she fell asleep. They had held hands and he had dropped her off to her apartment every day, often tucking her in as well.

Now with the time they had left together coming to an end, they were beginning to wonder about the future. Parth had felt that Ayesha was still holding some of herself back. It was almost like she was afraid to be hurt again.

He felt pained to think about it. She had eventually told him about her past, and he hated to think that he had only added to her hurt. He wished he could hold her close and care for her for the rest of his life.

"Ayesha..."

"Hmm..?"

"Please stay back with me."

Silence ensued.

Parth persisted, "What is it Ayesha? Do you not love me?"

"I don't think I've ever loved anyone else, Parth.."

"Then what is it?"

"I don't know. I'm scared. I... I worry that this might not last. This too might come to an end."

Parth got off the bench. With his knees on the ground, he sat in front of her and took her face in his hands. He looked into her eyes and said, "Ayesha, I've lost you once. I don't think I could bear to lose you again. So trust me when I say, that this time, I would never let go of you. If you fight with me, I'll hold on to you. If you doubt us, I'll still hold on to you. I want nothing more than to just be with you, girl."

Ayesha broke down then. She put her arms around him and cried. She cried for all those lost years, when they could have been together. She wept out of joy that someone loved her so much! What was she thinking?

Parth gently held her face in his hands again and kissed away her tears. He wished he could kiss away her fears too. He understood that she had seen too much pain from too many people, enough for a lifetime. He needed to earn her trust, but he needed her to be around him for that. She was going so far away. And he worried that if she had a change of mind, she might break all contact again.

He looked at her expectantly, but all she said was, "I need time to think."

~~❖~~

It was Ayesha's last night in Amsterdam. She had packed her bags, paid her rent and wound up the house. Parth was now waiting for her outside her apartment to take her out for dinner.

He had waited for an answer to his question, but all she had said was, "I need time to think." Parth was hurt, but he didn't want to show it. He decided to make the most of the evening.

When she stepped out in a blue and white evening dress, Parth drew his breath in and let it out slowly.

"Have I ever told you that you're beautiful, Ayesha..."

Ayesha smiled and gave him her hand. He took it and they turned to walk together.

Over dinner, she told him about her final meeting with the landlady, Mrs van Til. She was an old lady who had been quite enraptured with the fact that Ayesha was Indian. She loved listening to stories of India from Ayesha, and in turn narrated stories about her grandchildren.

Ayesha was to leave early the next morning and had promised to leave the key under the flower pot outside the house, as Mrs van Til would find it difficult to wake up and come over that early.

As they were paying the bill, Parth spoke up, "I have something to show you. Come along!"

Intrigued, Ayesha followed him out of the restaurant and down the road. She asked him twice where they were going, but Parth only smiled in return.

"You ask too many questions!" was his only retort.

She finally shrugged her shoulders and continued to banter away about her farewell party at college and the little gifts she had received from her students. She did return time and again to the same university to teach for a semester, but her students rarely remained the same.

"I love their zeal and enthusiasm for life. It somehow keeps me going as well."

Parth led her across the road and into a park she had not been in before. There was a canal flowing right through the park and the moonlight reflected in the water. They walked for a while, before running into a wall, about five feet high. Ayesha was just wondering what they were up to, when Parth said, "C'mon. I'll help you climb over the wall."

"Climb over?! But why?"

"You ask too many questions! And whatever happened to Ms Adventurous?"

She shook her head and looked up at the wall again to find a footing. Before she knew it, Parth had taken her in his arms and placed her on the wall! Ayesha jumped off over to the other side and Parth followed. They walked up a little hillock in silence. There was not a soul there.

"Where are we?" Ayesha asked.

"In the middle of nowhere... That's what I love about this place. When I want to be away from the entire world, I come here."

As they reached the tip of the hillock, Ayesha began to

see why Parth loved the spot so much. There were no trees on the hillock and one could look straight up at the million stars in the sky. It was dark where they were, but in the distance, the lights of the city shimmered all around them. It was absolutely quiet and peaceful. If one stayed completely still, you could even hear the light gush of the water in the canal.

They sat down on the grass. Looking up at the moon, Ayesha was taken back in time to those moonlit nights on the terrace of her roof, when she was just getting to know Parth. She had looked up at it then, as she had many other times, wondering if the man she would finally find and love was looking at the moon at the same time as her. She didn't know then, that he had been sitting right beside her.

She turned to look at Parth and saw him lying on the grass, gazing at the stars and the moon. She lay down next to him, putting her head on his shoulder, and looked back into the sky.

They lay like that for a long while, until Parth hoisted himself on his elbow and looked down into her eyes. He saw the moonlight reflected in them. If seven years back he had been unsure, he knew now with complete certainty that he was looking into the eyes of the woman he wanted to spend his life with.

She matched his gaze and the love in her eyes was unmistakable. Parth wanted to wake up to this sight every single morning for the rest of his life.

Gently, Parth lowered his lips to meet hers. He gave her a soft kiss, then pulled himself back to look at her. Her eyes were closed in wonder and she looked so sweet, that he couldn't resist kissing her again. This time she responded with a fervor that surprised him.

He felt her fingers in his hair, pulling him towards her. Parth's hands caressed her, going from her neck, along her arms, to her waist. His heart started beating faster as he felt her respond.

They kissed passionately, lost in their own world.

chapter 14

Ayesha felt pained every time she thought back to that last day together in Amsterdam, when Parth had dropped her off to the airport. He had insisted on an answer.

"Tell me Ayesha, what is wrong? I know you love me - I can see it, feel it. You know I love you. I always have. Why don't you want to see us together?"

"It's not that, Parth," Ayesha countered.

"What is it?"

"I just need some time to think. The last one month was beautiful, but I have to get away from you to think straight."

"Think about what?"

"Whether I want to marry you..." Parth had proposed marriage to her that last evening in the park, on the hillock. It had been enchanting- coming just after the passionate moments they had shared. She had held Parth's face tenderly in her hands, and requested him for some time. His face had fallen and she had felt cruel, but she could not make a hasty decision.

"You love me Ayesha?"

"Hmm.."

"Then why would you not want to marry me?"

Ayesha was beginning to feel driven against the wall. She had tried to leave then, but he had held her hand.

"I... I need to be sure that I can live with you without blaming you, Parth... You left me the first time. I have lived the last seven years remembering you and loving you. Where were you all these years? Did you try to find me and bring us together? And now that you chanced upon me, you want us to get married. I have spent too long agonising over you, Parth. I never blamed you until I thought you were with Naina, but now... I don't know. I don't understand. I need time to think..."

He had let her hand drop then. She had seen the look of pain on his face and known that she shouldn't have said what she had.

She was not sure whether he was to blame, but she had to be sure before she signed up for a life together. It would have been utterly unfair to live with him and with a nagging doubt about his commitment.

Parth had turned around and walked away then. Ayesha had felt heart-broken, but she had headed into the airport. She had turned around to see if he was looking at her, but he had disappeared.

He had disappeared into thin air.

It had been six months since then, and Ayesha was bereft with grief. On her return to London, she had spent a month thinking about their relationship. She had tried reaching him after that, but she couldn't find him.

His mobile number was unavailable. Someone else had responded on Parth's office desk number, only saying that Parth had left the company. He had not known where she could find him. Emails and messages went unanswered.

Ayesha had finally realised that if he had let her go the first time, she was to blame for this time. Worst of all, she couldn't forget that pained look she had seen last on his face, before he had left her life. She had hurt him, and she could not forgive herself for that.

Having completed her three-month assignment in London, Ayesha had returned to India to visit her parents. If they had noticed her forlorn look, they did not say anything about it. Luckily, neither did they mention the topic of marriage anymore.

It had struck Ayesha that she could go to his house in Ahmedabad. Would she find him there? His parents would know where he was. But what would she say to them? Did they know about Parth and her?

~~❖~~

As the months went by without her being able to make any contact with Parth, she decided to make that trip to Ahmedabad. She was still not sure what she would say to his parents, but she had to try. Ayesha had lost Parth due to her own thoughtlessness and it was now up to her to win him back. She could no longer find it in her heart to blame him after what she had done.

An overnight train brought her from Delhi to Ahmedabad. Vaguely familiar from her last visit, she found her way to her old home. As she got off the auto rickshaw, Ayesha gazed up at the common terrace of the two houses- the place where it had all started.

One finds love in the most unexpected of places; she mused, and then loses it in the most foolish of ways.

Someone else seemed to be living in her old house, but she was sure Parth's family was still living in the house next door. The line of Mercedes, BMWs and Audis were unmistakable.

It was only 9am in the morning, and Ayesha looked a mess after the overnight journey. She was wondering whether to approach the house or first check into a hotel, freshen up and return.

Just then, a young girl who looked just like Parth walked towards the house with a small dog on a leash. From the opposite end of the road, Ayesha watched her hand over the dog to the gardener, turn around and cross the street over to where she stood.

"Ayesha...?"

Ayesha was confused, but had to answer.

"Yes, that's me. But how do you know me?"

The girl smiled.

"My brother sketches you all the time. I'm among the privileged few who get to see his work."

She took a step forward and shook Ayesha's hand.

"I'm really glad you came."

"Piya?" Ayesha asked tentatively.

Parth had mentioned his sister, Piya, a couple of times. She was about a decade younger than Parth and still looked like a college-going girl. Her smile was infectious and her eyes reflected the same sincerity that Ayesha had noticed in Parth's eyes.

"Yes, that's me. C'mon, let's walk down the road. There's a new coffee shop that has opened up. They serve awesome cinnamon donuts!"

Ayesha nodded and walked with Piya. She only had a small overnight backpack with her and she carried that along. She was slightly relieved that she had been spared the awkwardness of walking into the house and explaining who she was to Parth's parents. At least Piya seemed to know about her.

"So how's your work coming along?" Piya asked.

"Good, thanks. I just returned to India to visit my parents.

I fly back to London next week. What about you? What do you do?"

"I'm doing my Masters at Delhi University. I'm visiting my parents too! I guess that's a lucky coincidence."

As they settled at a table outside the café, Piya flashed Ayesha a warm smile and Ayesha began to feel a little more comfortable. Moreover, Piya's mannerisms and expressions were a lot like Parth and somehow, that made her even more endearing.

Ayesha was suddenly reminded so acutely of the way Parth looked at her, touched her and laughed with her, that she couldn't help it when a few tears slid down her face.

chapter

15

"Oh, you poor thing," Piya came closer to her and held her. "Tell me, what happened?"

Ayesha suddenly broke down.

All this while, she had tried to be strong. She couldn't tell anyone what she had been going through. She had kept her agony to herself and now, suddenly, it all flowed out. "I... I lost him," she sobbed, "I'm such a fool!"

"Shh... shh... It's okay. He took a long time to make up his mind the first time. Now it's his turn to know what it feels like."

Ayesha looked up, wiping her tears hastily. "Do you... do you know about..."

"Yes, I do. After you had left the first time, Parth had visited me. I used to study in Nainital then. I'm much younger than him, but we have always been close enough to tell each other everything. He was torn between Naina and you. She had been in his life and he loved her, but whatever you and he shared over that one week, shook his life enough to confuse him. I couldn't of course advise him in this case. He had to take the decision himself, and he decided not to betray Naina... Let me call for some breakfast first. Give me a minute."

Ayesha composed herself, while Piya placed the order.

She was listening to Parth's side of the story for the first time. Even when they had met in Amsterdam, he had not discussed it. All he had said was that Naina had decided to move on and had married someone else.

Piya turned her attention back to Ayesha and continued, "They got engaged soon after you left and then Parth's employers moved him to a small place in Andhra Pradesh. A year went by and then two. Naina must have realised that Parth's heart was not in their relationship. He worked like a madman at the factory. He loved his job no doubt, but only I knew that he was trying hard to forget you at the same time. Eventually, Naina broke off the engagement and married a colleague."

She looked into the distance, as if recollecting the events.

"At first Parth reacted by throwing himself at his work even more than before," Piya went on. "He moved to Malaysia and we didn't see him for a year, except when I visited him for a couple of days once. That's when he told me that he had moved heaven and earth trying to find you. He just wanted to know where you were and how you were doing. Your parents had moved away by then, and he couldn't find a clue about you. He had to assume that by then you were married and settled. He was in grief, but the last thing he wanted to do was upset your world."

Ayesha felt tears slipping down her face. She had blamed him for not being committed enough, not trying to find her, and all that while, he had been trying to protect her and the world he thought she had created around her.

"When he finally found you in Amsterdam last year, he was happy beyond belief!" Piya continued. "He told me he was going to bring you home and introduce you to our parents. He had said he would leave his job, if required, to adjust with your lifestyle and work. He was planning life together with you, but I think he didn't say any of this, because he was waiting for you to make up your mind."

Ayesha nodded sadly. She wondered if things would have been different, had he voiced these thoughts to her then. Why hadn't she seen all that love in him? Why had she ever doubted him?

"When you left, you said something to him. I don't know what it was. All I know is that it broke him. Every time I asked him what had happened, he only said that you did not trust him. You guys had miraculously found each other after so long, and I couldn't believe that it had all gone downhill after that. I had told him that girls sometimes read things more emotionally and he should speak to you again, but he didn't want to upset you anymore."

"Where is he now?" Ayesha asked in a small voice.

"Rotterdam"

"Where is that?"

"It is a small town about two hours outside of Amsterdam."

"What is he doing there?"

"He left his job in Amsterdam after you left. He lives in Rotterdam and sketches."

Ayesha was quiet for a while. Then in a firm voice, she said, "I'll go and find him."

Piya nodded with a smile, pulled a napkin from the table and wrote down Parth's address and phone number.

"Would he want to see me?" Ayesha asked.

"I don't know if he knows the answer to that, but I know one thing for sure. Nothing would make him happier than to see you!"

Ayesha hugged Piya and said, "Thank you for everything!"

"You guys have waited too long for each other. You deserve to be together now."

chapter 16

Ayesha knew exactly what she wanted from life this time. No more being confused. She took some decisive actions. She called up her office at London and requested for an extension of her leave by a week. She then canceled her ticket to London, which was scheduled for the next week, and booked one for Amsterdam instead.

She wasn't sure what to tell her parents, so she just said that work was taking her to Amsterdam, instead of the UK. She packed her bags and set out in search of the love she had found, lost, found once more and lost yet again.

She felt like an incredible fool for all the wasted time, but she thanked God for at least bringing Parth into her life. Without him, her life was direction-less and meaningless. All those years they had been apart, when she thought he was settled with Naina- even then it had always been about him. She used to think about him all the time.

Through the long flight, Ayesha remained fidgety. As she approached her destination, she became increasingly anxious. Was Parth angry with her? Had he changed his mind about her? Would he be happy to see her? Why had he gone to Rotterdam? She had his number, but she hadn't called him. She felt that she needed to see him face-to-face.

Landing at Schipol airport, Ayesha boarded the Inter-city train to Rotterdam. The journey was to take about two hours. As the Dutch countryside passed by, Ayesha couldn't help but feel enchanted with all that she saw.

The fields everywhere were specked with beautiful daisy cows - black and white. Windmills dotted the horizon. Little cottages and pretty houses came along the way. She also saw many small and large churches.

Ayesha looked at everything with new eyes. She was happy that she was going to see Parth again, very soon. She kept thinking of life ahead- with Parth by her side. They would live in a little cottage too, maybe in The Netherlands itself. They would walk hand-in-hand, sharing life, chattering away like they had right from the time they met. She kept shaking her head at what she had almost lost and she kept her fingers crossed that all would be fine hereon.

On arrival at Rotterdam Centraal Station, Ayesha deboarded the train and headed outside the station. She hitched a ride on a taxi and shared Parth's address with the chauffeur. She was feeling impatient to meet him and could not get herself to find a hotel first. After a twenty minute ride, the taxi came to a halt in a peaceful residential area. Pulling her bag behind her, Ayesha slowly made her way inside, following the numbers.

Despite being February, the weather was still quite cold and it started getting dark by around 6pm. Battling the cold winds, Ayesha wished she was wearing her mittens and cap. About a hundred yards later, she came to a halt outside a little studio apartment on the ground floor.

Clutching the napkin on which Piya had scribbled the address, Ayesha re-confirmed that she had reached her destination. To her utter dismay, the house was locked and dark. She sat on the pavement opposite the house wondering what to do.

She wasn't even sure that Parth actually lived here. What if he had moved since Piya gave her the address? What if he were outside town, traveling maybe? The minutes ticked away and at 7pm, Ayesha got up and headed back to the main road.

She needed to pull out her heavy woolens from her bag and for that she first needed to check into a hotel.

~~❖~~

As the soft light of dawn fell on Ayesha's face, she woke up. For a minute, she felt disoriented. Where was she?

Remembering that she had found a hotel in Rotterdam and checked-in last night, she realised that she must have dozed off while waiting for the dinner to come. The jet-lag had set in and she had slept through the night. Feeling ravenously hungry, she called room service once again and placed a request for breakfast.

An hour later, Ayesha had done a few stretches, taken a shower and had a hearty breakfast. Putting on warm woolens and a big red coat, along with mittens and a cap, Ayesha set out once again to the address Piya had given her. She once again reached to find the house locked.

That was when Ayesha remembered that Piya had also given her a phone number. Sitting on the pavement once again, she pulled out the number and stared at it. She didn't have a phone. Should she head to the nearest market and get a local phone connection?

Just then Ayesha saw Parth approaching the house. He was accompanied by a pretty girl, seemingly Dutch. Ayesha wondered if he was dating this girl. Suddenly, she didn't want to be seen. Pulling her cap low, she turned slightly away and hoped he wouldn't recognise her. Parth and the girl were busy in an animated conversation. They stepped into the house and closed the door.

Ayesha stared at the door in dismay. Had she lost him again? She had come all the way, only to find him with another girl! At that moment, the door opened again and the girl stepped out holding a book in her hand. She must have come to borrow this, Ayesha hoped! The girl kissed Parth on the cheek and then waved at him as she left.

He was just turning to re-enter the house, when his eyes fell on Ayesha, difficult to miss in the bright red coat! She was staring at him and he saw a mix of emotions in her eyes - hope, dismay, confusion...

After a few moments, Parth sighed, closed the door and crossed over to where Ayesha was sitting. He joined her at the pavement, sitting close but not touching her.

Just his proximity triggered powerful emotions in Ayesha, as she remembered that last night they had been together on the hillock. She closed her eyes, remembering his kisses and wished he would take her into his arms right there.

Parth, however, sat silently, looking at Ayesha.

"What are you doing in Rotterdam?" Ayesha asked.

He smiled.

"You've always had so many questions. Shouldn't I be asking you that? How did you find me?"

"Piya..."

"You went home?!" Parth was surprised.

"Hmm... I needed to find you... I'm sorry, Parth. Could you possibly forgive me for what I said that day?"

"Do you still feel that way?" he asked.

Ayesha shook her head violently.

"No! I was confused and foolish. Piya told me everything. You... you've loved me all along... She said you didn't contact me for my sake, but you tried to find me. I'm sorry, Parth!"

"You don't need to apologise. I goofed up too. Come inside..."

They stood up and walked into his apartment. It was warm and cozy inside. Ayesha was stunned to see the walls of the room full of sketches of herself, staring back at her! The room was full of easels and large sketches, many of them portraying her.

There was one of her lying down on some grass, under the moonlight, with an unmistakable expression of love in her eyes. She had always marveled at the way Parth could capture intense emotions in people's eyes.

"Why did you disappear?" she asked.

"You didn't trust me. And that was something I couldn't live with. We couldn't be together while you blamed me in your heart."

Tears slipped out of Ayesha's eyes. She slowly took his hand in hers and said, "I never ever want to lose you again, Parth."

He put his arm around her and pulled her towards him. She put her head on his shoulder and leaned in.

"I told you, Ayesha. I promised you. I'll never love anyone else. I was yours from that moment on the terrace when I first saw you. Only I didn't know it then..."

She raised her head to look at him.

He gazed back at her.

Then lowered his lips and sealed his promise with a kiss.

About the Author

BORN
MARCH 02, 1988

Stay updated about Piyushi's latest works online:

https://www.facebook.com/**piyushi**dhir**author**

https://twitter.com/**Piyushi**_s

http://www.amazon.com/**Piyushi**-Dhir/e/B00UDICBGK

https://plus.google.com/+**Piyushi**Dhir/posts

goodreads https://www.goodreads.com/author/show/13500518.**Piyushi**_Dhir

PIYUSHI DHIR is an author, blogger and traveler, who resides in Ivory Coast, Africa. A nomad at heart, she has travelled across 4 continents, 12 countries and 50 cities so far. She loves to discover new places and capture the hues of life with her pen.

Before donning her current avatar as a writer, Piyushi worked as a Human Resources Manager at Citibank for a couple of years in India. She is an English Literature graduate from Lady Shriram College, New Delhi and has completed her Masters' in Business Administration from Management Development Institute, India and Rotterdam School of Management, The Netherlands.

The daughter of an Indian Air Force fighter pilot, Piyushi travelled the length and breadth of India during her childhood. The exposure to various cultures and places developed in her an innate curiosity about people, their behaviours and psychologies. A passion for books that began at an early stage with a compulsive reading habit, eventually led her to pen down her own stories and novels.

Her first novel, 'In Search of Love', was published in 2014; followed by 'I'm Yours, The Next Time' in 2015. 'Enmeshed Evermore' is her latest publication, a novella based on the story of 'In Search of Love'. This book is currently available on her website for free download.

You can read more about Piyushi Dhir on:

www.**piyushi**dhir.com

You can also write to the author:

piyushi.dhir@gmail.com

Crowd-funders

(names listed alphabetically)

Aanchal Mehra

Amit Tirpude

Arjun Dutt

Avinash Kohli

Chirag Sidana

Diti Bhadra

Garima Dhir

Gaurav Dhir

Kavya V

Mani Bhushan

Priyanka Pardasani

Purna Banerjee

Rajesh Sobti

Ravi Bharti

Samant Sikka

Sanghita Roychaudhury

Sanhita Haldar

Shuchi Tomer

Snehil Gautam

Stephenie Mascarenhas

Sunita Chopra

Susovan Ray

Swati Verma

Vaibhav Roy

Vidyasagar Vajapeyazula

in search of LOVE

Piyushi Dhir

Did you like the book?

Email your
questions, experiences, and suggestions
to the author at

piyushi.dhir@gmail.com

Enmeshed Evermore - A Novella

Published 2015

An unexpected encounter between two people who had once been in love. Parth and Ayesha meet seven years after their first tryst in Ahmedabad, but this time they are both married... to other people.

Will their dormant feelings for each other resurface? Will they risk everything they have, to bring back what they had buried before?

To all the readers of *In Search of Love* –

Wondered what would have happened if Parth had gone ahead and married Naina? What if Ayesha's parents had finally found her a suitable match?

Enmeshed Evermore explores a different ending to Ayesha and Parth's story. A must-read for anyone who read and enjoyed *In Search of Love.*

I'm Yours, The Next Time

Published 2015

Yet another session is starting at School of Global Management. Join a bunch of MBA aspirants as they embark on a journey of a lifetime.

Piya: Hip, happy, vivacious, ambitious. A Goa-girl, she lands up at SGM to pursue a Business School degree that will take her places. She is eager to embrace life until she realizes what it has in store for her: a shattered heart and a broken existence.

Kartik: Athletic, handsome, the centre of all female attention, Kartik however wants none of it. He has been betrayed once and has vowed to remain unsaddled, until he meets her and starts losing his heart, little by little.

Rohan: Laid back, relaxed and cool as a cucumber, to him SGM is all about bike rides, fun and friends. Never one to get entangled, Rohan's life is altered by one girl he is ready to do anything for.

Join Piya, Kartik, Rohan, Tamanna and Nitya on a roller-coaster ride, as SGM brings a lot more tumult to their lives than they had bargained for.

In the midst of heart-breaks, conspiracies and accidents, friendships are formed and relationships forged. Will some of these last until the next lifetime?

more books by Piyushi Dhir

"

Reader Reviews...

'In Search of Love' is the first book written by Piyushi Dhir, who has put her defence background (daughter of an ex Air Force fighter pilot) and the academic stint in Netherlands, to good use in building the plot to this romantically gripping story.

Though the theme is as old as humanity itself, she has given a refreshingly contemporary perspective to the subject of love and relationships. An unputdownable and extremely well written book that leaves a lump in your throat.

A must read, both, for those who are romantically inclined, and those who are not!

- RAJESH SOBTI (December 28, 2014)

'In Search of Love' is a delicately handled romance novel by Piyushi Dhir. It brings out the fact that all stumbling blocks that hurl into a relationship between two people, actually pile up somewhere to become stepping stones to a beautiful life they are meant to share together. The narrative of the story is fluid, sprinkled with graceful verses every now and then. The journey of the protagonists through some fascinating cities across the world like Ahmedabad, London and Amsterdam, only to discover that wherever they went, it was always love waiting at the final destination ,to take them into its arms, is something that will surely resonate with all readers, especially girls who may be delighted to find a friend in Ayesha.

- SHWETA RAVI SHANKAR (March 30, 2015)

Must read!. Excellent work by the author!

- SANIYA MALIM (April 7, 2016)

Nice chic lit good romantic story. I could not put down had to finish in one hit. I liked the Indian connections.

- LUISA (May 21, 2015)

'In Search of Love', a romantic novel by Piyushi Dhir, is an adoring description of Parth and Ayesha's love story. The book provides a modern day outlook to the story; however, a simple yet touching verse here or there gives it a very dreamy touch.

The characters in the plot felt real and relatable, suited more for young readers. The book manages to take you by surprise without giving any spoilers.

Simple yet sweet, this book keeps you hooked till the last page.

- GARIMA (May 25, 2015)

An endearing, straight from the heart narration. The author steps aside to explore the sometimes iceberg like nature of love, where what is evident often belies the depth and size of that which is not evident. Keep it ready on your Kindle, for the next time you have a couple of hours to spare.

- VK THAKUR (October 26, 2015)

"

in search of
LOVE